Critical acclaim for Scott Turow

LIMITATIONS

'Fascinating . . . has the same elegant style,
the same skilled storytelling [as *Presumed Innocent*]
and raises some thought-provoking issues'
Sunday Telegraph

'Turow sets up [the story] with consummate
expertise. The characters are skilfully portrayed,
the plotting is deft and the writing a cut
above John Grisham's'
Sunday Times

'Wide in moral scope and brimming with humanity'
Daily Mirror Book of the Week

'Scott Turow does legal thrillers better than
anyone else, and writes with a wonderful precision
and style that lifts *Limitations* far beyond the
norm of the genre. Highly recommended'
Irish Independent

ORDINARY HEROES

'Turow is a serious, rewarding writer.
Ordinary Heroes is a page-turner, but also
an unburdening that is worth reading'
The Times

'Part-mystery, part-thriller,
this is a quietly powerful piece of fiction'
Observer

'The pace never slackens and neither
does the moral tension . . . gripping'
Daily Mirror

'A novel worth reading, leaving the reader
with a lasting sense of the corrosive effects of
war on even the most civilized souls'
Washington Post

REVERSIBLE ERRORS

'Demonstrates why Turow remains head-and-shoulders above others in the legal thriller genre he created . . . a humane examination of flawed people and an engrossing mystery. Terrific'
Observer

'Absorbing and unsettling'
Times Literary Supplement

'An intelligent, ambitious novel and one, crucially, with something to say'
Mail on Sunday

'Turow is a wonderful stylist . . . He is also a brilliant chronicler of contemporary America'
Sunday Times

'When it comes to courtroom drama, Turow blows even Grisham out of the water . . . A novel that'll have you chomping at the bit from beginning to end'
Daily Mirror

ULTIMATE PUNISHMENT

'The strength of his book is that it is the product
of genuine open-mindedness rather than of an
opinion firmly held from the very outset . . . his book
makes a case against capital punishment all
the stronger for not being strident'
Sunday Telegraph

'Readable and fascinating'
Cherie Booth

'Scott Turow, with the consummate skill
of the thriller writer, portrays the reasons why
a society might struggle over the question
of capital punishment'
Financial Times

'Poignant and hugely powerful musing on America
and the death penalty . . . its spare and elegant prose
will leave no side in the debate feeling short-
changed . . . Turow never hectors or judges and yet
effortlessly steers the reader to the close'
Daily Telegraph

LIMITATIONS

Scott Turow is the internationally renowned author of six bestselling novels about the law, from *Presumed Innocent* to *Reversible Errors*. His most recent novel, *Ordinary Heroes*, was a critically acclaimed thriller set in the Second World War. He has also written a work of non-fiction, *Ultimate Punishment*, which centres on the death penalty. He lives with his family outside Chicago, where he is a partner in the international law firm of Sonnenschein Nath & Rosenthal.

ALSO BY SCOTT TUROW

FICTION

Presumed Innocent

The Burden of Proof

Pleading Guilty

The Laws of Our Fathers

Personal Injuries

Reversible Errors

Ordinary Heroes

NON-FICTION

*One L: The Turbulent True Story of a First Year
at Harvard Law School*

*Ultimate Punishment: A Lawyer's Reflections on
Dealing with the Death Penalty*

PAN BOOKS

SCOTT TUROW

LIMITATIONS

PAN BOOKS

First published in the United States 2006 by Picador
an imprint of Farrar, Straus and Giroux
New York, USA

First published in Great Britain 2006 by Picador

This paperback edition published 2007 by Pan Books
an imprint of Pan Macmillan Ltd
Pan Macmillan, 20 New Wharf Road, London N1 9RR
Basingstoke and Oxford
Associated companies throughout the world
www.panmacmillan.com

ISBN 978-0-330-45115-4

Commissioned by and first published by
The New York Times Magazine

The right of Scott Turow to be identified as the
author of this work has been asserted by him in accordance
with the Copyright, Designs and Patents Act 1988.

This is a work of fiction. All of the characters, organizations,
and events portrayed in this novel are either products of
the author's imagination or are used fictitiously.

3 5 7 9 8 6 4 2

A CIP catalogue record for this book is available from
the British Library.

Printed and bound in Great Britain by
Mackays of Chatham plc, Chatham, Kent

Visit **www.panmacmillan.com** to read more about all our books
and to buy them. You will also find features, author interviews and
news of any author events, and you can sign up for e-newsletters
so that you're always first to hear about our new releases.

For Vivian and Richard

Few love to hear the sins they love to act.

SHAKESPEARE,
Pericles, Act I, Scene I

LIMITATIONS

I

THE ARGUMENT

"May it please the court," booms Jordan Sapperstein from the podium. "This case must be reversed. Your Honors have no choice."

Seated behind the elevated walnut bench a dozen feet away, Judge George Mason suppresses an impulsive wince at Sapperstein's excesses. The judge is seldom reluctant to let lawyers know when their claims are unpersuasive, but making faces, as his father warned him when he was a boy in Virginia long ago, is simply rude.

The truth is that George Mason recoils even

more from the case, *People v. Jacob Warnovits et al.*, than from the celebrated attorney beginning his oral argument. Before he was elected to the bench, at age forty-seven, George was a criminal defense lawyer, perpetually engrossed in his warring feelings— loathing, amusement, intrigue, envy—about those who broke the rules. Yet from the instant the Court of Appeals' docket department randomly placed him on *Warnovits* five weeks ago, he has been uneasy about the assignment. He has found it uncharacteristically difficult to read the briefs or view the record of the trial in the Kindle County Superior Court, where nineteen months ago, the four young defendants were convicted of criminal sexual assault and given the mandatory minimum sentence of six years. Now the judge thinks what he has every time the matter has come reluctantly to mind: hard cases make bad law.

As the senior member of the three-judge panel, Judge Mason, in his inky robe, occupies the center spot on the long bench between his two colleagues. Judge Summerset Purfoyle, with his time-engraved pecan face and a sponge of white hair, is perhaps more regally handsome now than in his days as a successful soul balladeer. The other judge, Nathan Koll, small and stout, his plump jowls like a croissant beneath his chin, eyes Sapperstein from his first words with a dark, merciless look.

Beyond the lawyers in the well of the court, the security officers have fit onto the walnut pews as many as possible of the spectators who lined up at the courtroom door, leaving the air close on a warm day at the start of June. In the front row, the reporters and sketch artists hastily record what they can. Behind them the onlookers—law students, court buffs, friends of the defendants, and supporters of the victim—are now intent, after having shifted through three civil cases argued before the same panel earlier in the morning. Even the stateliness of the appellate courtroom, with its oxblood pillars of marble rising two stories to the vaulted ceiling and the gilded rococo details on the furnishings, cannot fully dampen the high-wattage current of controversy that has long enlivened the *Warnovits* case, which has taken on complex meanings for thousands of people who know nothing about the legal principles at stake and not much more about the underlying facts.

The victim of the crime is Mindy DeBoyer, although her name, as an alleged rape victim, is never used in the frequent public accounts. More than seven years ago, in March 1999, Mindy was fifteen and a member of the rowdy throng at a house party for the Glen Brae High School boys' ice hockey team. Earlier that day, Glen Brae had finished second in the state. The players were sore — from the pounding of six games in six days and from failing after coming so close to the state title — and the celebration in the home of the team co-captain, Jacob Warnovits, whose parents had flown off to a wedding in New York, was out of control from the start. Mindy DeBoyer, by her own testimony, 'got hammered beyond belief' on the combination of rum and a pill provided by Warnovits and somehow ended up passed out in his room.

Warnovits claimed he had discovered her there and took Mindy's position, like Goldilocks in the bed of one of the three bears, as a proposition. The jury clearly rejected that explanation, probably because Warnovits also invited three other team members to join him in violating the young woman, who was unconscious and lifeless as a rag doll.

6

Warnovits captured each assault on videotape, often employing the camera in a grotesque fashion that would startle even a pornographer. The soundtrack, a vile screed from Warnovits, ended after more than fifty minutes with his warnings to his friends to get Mindy out of there and 'don't say jack.'

When she awoke at about 5:00 A.M. amid the lingering reek from the empty cans and ashes in the Warnovitses' living room, Mindy DeBoyer had no idea what had occurred. A sexual novice, although not uninitiated, she realized she'd had rough treatment, and she noticed that her skirt was on backward. Yet she had no memory of any of the night's late events. After sneaking home, she phoned other kids she'd seen at the party, but no one could recall who Mindy had gone off with. Speaking to her best friend, Vera Hartal, Mindy DeBoyer wondered if she might even have been raped. But she was fifteen and not eager to involve an adult, or admit where she had been. She healed in her own time and said nothing.

And so life marched on. The four boys graduated from high school and went to college, as did Mindy two and a half years later. Feeling safer with time,

Jacob Warnovits could not resist occasionally entertaining his fraternity brothers with the tape. One
freshman pledge, Michael Willets, turned out to be
close to the DeBoyer family, and after a lengthy
conversation with his sister, he tipped the police,
who arrived at the fraternity house with a search
warrant. Mindy DeBoyer reviewed the videotape in
horror, and Warnovits and the three other young
men were indicted in quick order on January 14,
2003.

As George Mason views the case, the principal
legal question is the statute of limitations, which
under state law would ordinarily bar bringing felony
charges more than three years after the crime. But
the grinding social issue is that Mindy DeBoyer is
black. She is well-to-do, like the boys who assaulted
her, but her parents, a lawyer and an MBA, could
not keep from wondering publicly, in their initial
agitation, whether a young white woman would
have been treated the same way in Glen Brae, a
suburban town to which integration came
grudgingly.

The racial charges raised the volume in Glen

Brae. Families close to the four boys proclaimed that their lives were being ruined long after the fact for a crime from which the victim had not really suffered. They implied that race alone was causing men to be punished for the misdeeds of children. The sharp disputes between neighbors boiled over into the press, where the DeBoyers' views have clearly prevailed. Most accounts portray the defendants as spoiled rich boys who nearly escaped after a night of bestial fun in the slave cabin, even though not one of the many ugly terms the boys had applied to Mindy on the tape involved any mention of her race.

The substantial questions presented by the young men's appeal have allowed them to remain free on bond, and all four, now in their midtwenties, are beside the journalists in the front spectators' row. The fate of each is in the hands of Jordan Sapperstein, in a cream suit with heavy black pinstripes, who is gesticulating often and using his crinkled gray pageboy for emphasis. Judge Mason has never fully decoded whatever it is a human being is saying about himself when he sports a hairdo borrowed from Gorgeous George, but Sapperstein is what Patrice, the judge's wife, is apt in her moods to refer to as an LFT—lawyer from television.

A Californian, Sapperstein made his name twenty years ago, while a law professor at Stanford, with two stunning victories in the U.S. Supreme Court. He has remained a legal celebrity ever since, because of his willingness to puff himself into a state of agitation for thirty seconds whenever the red light glows above a TV camera. He is always turning up on CNN, *Meet the Press*, Court TV, so ubiquitous you half-expect him in the background when you video-record your niece's soccer game. The desperate families of the Glen Brae Four are rumored to have paid him several hundred thousand dollars to take on this appeal.

With some panels, George supposes that Sapperstein's notoriety might be a plus, providing cover for a judge inclined to reverse. But not here. Sapperstein's prominence has been a call to combat for George's colleague Nathan Koll. Koll, who left his position as an esteemed faculty member at Easton Law School to take a five-year interim appointment on the appellate court, prefers to treat attorneys as if they were his students, exuberantly pummeling them with sly hypothetical questions aimed at undermining their positions. Wags have long called this style of Socratic classroom interrogation 'the game only one can play,' and here too there is no winning with Nathan. The truth is that, for him, each case, no matter what the actual subject matter, presents the same issue: proving he is the smartest lawyer in the room. Or perhaps the universe. George is uncertain where the boundary falls on Nathan's sense of grandeur.

If nothing else, with his beerhouse voice and squinty inquisitorial style, Koll makes good theater, and he tears into Sapperstein not long after the lawyer begins his oral argument with a quotation from an exalted legal commentator, spiced, in turn, with the words of the U.S. Supreme Court.

"Statutes of limitations on felony prosecutions, which 'are found and approved in all systems of enlightened jurisprudence,' implicitly reflect a legislative judgment that the moral gravity of an offense can be measured by the urgency with which punishment is pursued. 'The general experience of mankind' is that true crimes 'are not usually allowed to remain neglected,'" Sapperstein declaims.

"Hardly, hardly," Koll answers immediately. Even seated, he reminds George of a linebacker ready to tackle, hunched forward, his stocky hands spread wide as if to hinder any effort to evade him. "Limitations periods, Mr. Sapperstein, arise fundamentally from worries that memories weaken and evidence is dispersed over time. Which should not concern us when there is a videotape of the offense."

Sapperstein will not back down, and the academic jousting between the judge and the lawyer continues for several minutes, two legal peacocks spreading their feathers. In George's mind, the impressions of noted legal scholars about why Anglo-American jurisprudence favors statutes of limitations count for very little. The only operative fact is that the legislature in this state voted for one. As a judge, George takes it as his principal task simply to resolve any doubts about the meaning of the words the lawmakers used.

Ordinarily, he might interrupt with that observation, but on balance, he prefers to keep his distance from this case. Besides, it's seldom an easy matter to get a remark in edgewise when you sit with Nathan Koll. Judge Purfoyle, on George's right, has several questions written on his yellow pad, but Koll has yet to yield the floor, despite several gentlemanly efforts by Summer.

In any event, George's attention is soon drawn to the thumping entrance into the courtroom of one of his two law clerks, Cassandra Oakey. Cassie cannot go anywhere without causing a distraction: she is too forceful, tall and attractive, and entirely unschooled in self-restraint. But as she charges forward to the clerks' table at the far side of the courtroom, George realizes that she is not, as he might have expected, simply late. Cassie casts her large, dark eyes urgently toward him, and he sees she is holding a note. And with that a little wrinkle of terror creases the judge's heart. Patrice, he thinks. This happens to George Mason several times each day. Lost in the professional issues that have always overwhelmed him like a siren call, he feels shocked and selfish when the recollection smashes home: Patrice has cancer. She had been hospitalized for two days now for post-operative radioactive treatments, and his immediate fear is that something has gone wrong.

Cassie creeps close enough to get the folded paper to Marcus, George's white-whiskered bailiff, who passes it up. But the subject, George finds, is his own well-being, not his wife's. Dineesha, his assistant, has written:

> *We have heard again from #1. Marina would like to brief you on what she found out from the FBI but has to leave the building for the day at 1:00 P.M. Any chance you could put off the judges' conference for half an hour to see her?*

George lifts a temporizing finger in Cassie's direction. Koll has now taken to battering Sapperstein about his other principal argument, which is that the videotape of the assault was too graphic and inflammatory to have been played for the jury without substantial editing, especially of the boys' priapic displays to one another and Warnovits's gynecological inspections of Mindy with the camera.

"You are not contending," Koll says, "that the videotape, at least in some form, was inadmissible?"

"The videotape, Your Honor, as the jury saw it, should not have come into evidence."

"But only on the grounds that some elements were unduly prejudicial?"

Sapperstein has been in enough courtrooms to sense a trap of some kind, but his evasions only intensify Koll's efforts to steamroll him.

Enough, George thinks. He looks to the clerks' table. There John Banion, the judge's other law clerk, has his finger on the buttons that control the three tiny warning lights atop the lectern, which indicate how much time for argument a lawyer has left. Currently, the orange lamp in the middle is aglow in front of Sapperstein. Banion, a doughy figure in his early forties, is often referred to behind his back by the other law clerks as 'the Droid' because he is remote as a hermit. But for years John has proven perfectly attuned to the judge's professional needs, and George drops his chin no more than an inch before John snaps on the red light signaling that Sapperstein's time is up.

"Thank you, Mr. Sapperstein," George says, cutting him off midsentence.

At the farther counsel table, nearer the clerks, the acting Kindle County Prosecuting Attorney, Tommy Molto, rises with a mess of papers in his hands to respond for the state. Asking for a second, George covers his microphone, a black bud on a black stalk, so he can confer privately first with Purfoyle, then Koll. Koll can't quite summon an agreeable expression but, like Purfoyle, grants George, as the presiding judge, the courtesy of a half-hour reprieve before the conference that normally would immediately follow the last argument. There the three judges will decide the cases they have heard this morning and assign among themselves the writing of the court's opinions.

"Tell Dineesha I'll see Marina," the judge says to Cassie after waving her up. In a crouch beside the judge's tall leather chair, Cassie is ready to depart, but George detains her. "What did number 1 say?"

Her brown eyes shift, and she gives her straight blond Dutch boy cut a toss in the interval.

"Just the same junk," she finally whispers.

"More wishes for my health and happiness?" George asks, wondering if the joke sounds brave or foolhardy.

"Really," she says.

But her reluctance about the message is provocative, and he circles his hand, asking for more.

"He, she, it, they—whoever it is sent a link," Cassie responds.

"A link?"

"To a Web site."

"What Web site?"

Cassie openly frowns. "It's called **Death Watch**," she answers.

2

#1

Judge George Mason is in the final year of a decade-long term on the State Court of Appeals for the Third Appellate District, an area principally composed of Kindle County. The chance to run for the appellate court had unexpectedly arisen only a year after he had been elected a Superior Court judge, presiding over a criminal courtroom downstairs in this same building, the Central Branch Courthouse. Many friends had discouraged him from considering the higher court, predicting he would find this life isolated and passive after a career on the front lines of trial combat, but the job—hearing arguments, reflecting on briefs and precedents, writing opinions—has suited him. To George Mason, the law has always posed the fundamental riddles life has asked him to solve.

In Virginia, law had been a family tradition, going back to his great namesake, the fabled American founder George Mason IV—the real George Mason, as the judge will always think of him. During George's years as an undergraduate in Charlottesville, a legal career was yet another of the many ponderous expectations his parents had placed upon him that he was determined to escape. With his degree in hand, he fled here, spending two years as an ordinary seaman on a coal freighter, a job that provided an alternative to Vietnam. His vessel sailed up the river Kindle and around the Great Lakes, and in his solitary hours on watch, when duty required him to contemplate the limitless waters as vast as the adult life that lay before him, he was shocked to find himself preoccupied with the intense questions of right and wrong, justice and power that had been parsed each night at his father's dinner table. At the end of his tour, he was eager to enroll at Easton Law

School here, becoming a Deputy State Defender after graduation. He loved the ragged extremes of crime, which took him so far from what he had been born to, and yet it was the patina of the Southern gentleman that abetted his success. With his gold-buttoned blazer, penny loafers, and gentle drawl, he seemed to cast a spell over the courtroom, as if his presence assured everyone—cops and judges and prosecutors and court personnel—that none of them belonged to the world of hurt and rage and ignorance that propelled these crimes. He alone knew that his performance was a parody.

So he had continued, not quite of this place yet surely not of the one he'd left. Popular with colleagues, he was elected President of the Kindle County Bar Association in the late 1980s. He remained successful and respected, but never the ultimate lawyer of choice in this town, where his friend Sandy Stern would forever be called first in a complicated criminal case. As George had wearied of practice, he found himself idly attracted to the ambition that had eluded his father: to be a judge. It was a wan hope, given the open disdain he'd always shown for the oily dealings of the party leaders who controlled such matters. He assumed he had damned himself forever when he agreed late in 1992 to represent a lawyer turned federal witness whose secret tape recordings led to the conviction of six judges and nine attorneys in a bribery scandal that burned through the Kindle County Superior Court. Instead, in one of those demonstrations of life's perpetual defiance of expectations, George found himself regarded as the very emblem of lawyerly independence, begged to run by the party powers, who were desperate to meet the outcry for reform. He led the judicial ballot in 1994, a success that leapfrogged him over dozens of more experienced candidates when a seat opened on the appellate court for the 1996 election.

Assuming George wants to keep his job, a yes-no question will appear this November on the County ballot: "Should George Thomson Mason be retained for another ten-year term as a justice of the appellate court?" Now and then, reading the record of a trial, he yearns to pick apart a weaseling witness again on cross-examination, and he frequently regrets the restrictions of a public salary. Occasionally, there are moments—when he longs to curse

out the umps at Trappers Park or must respond
stone-faced to certain jokes—that he feels caged by
the proprieties of the role he's taken on. Yet until
Patrice's illness, he had no doubt that he would
stand for retention, which he is nearly certain to
win. His candidacy papers are due in a matter of
weeks, but he has been waiting to file, just in case
life deals out more surprises.

Now, with his robe across his arm, George
sweeps into his chambers, a baronial space of high
ceilings and dark crown moldings. The oral argument in *Warnovits* came to an unsettling conclusion, with Nathan Koll engaged in more
grandstanding. The judge is just as happy to escape
for half an hour before confronting his colleagues
in conference.

In the outer office, Dineesha, the judge's assistant, is at work at her large desk. She hands him
several phone message slips—most requests that
George add a ceremonial presence to various public
events—but there is only one communication of
interest to him at the moment.

"So what did my favorite correspondent have to
say for himself this morning?" he asks.

Since this business with #1 started about three weeks ago, Dineesha has taken to screening his e-mail, so that Court Security can be alerted as quickly as possible about new developments. Calm and dignified, Dineesha has been attending to George in his professional life for close to twenty years, selflessly following him to the public sector from the plummier confines of private practice. Now she wobbles her stiff jet hairdo, a daily monument to the tensile strength of the polymers in her hair spray.

"Judge, you don't need to bother with this. With number 1," says Dineesha quietly, "it's all number two." Humor, especially anything remotely off-color, is uncharacteristic, and he takes her contained smile as a sign of outrage on his behalf.

Nobody in chambers has known how to refer to whoever is trying to unsettle the judge. 'The stalker' was George's initial term, but that gave too much credit to someone who really has no physical manifestation. Avenger. Nemesis. The Crank or The Crackpot. Irony became the default position. The message writer was referred to as the judge's #1 fan, and soon after that simply as #1.

George does not know if he is exhibiting strength of character by examining these messages or just irresistible curiosity. His excuse to himself is that sooner or later something will clue him to the sender's identity. Dineesha makes a face but opens today's e-mail while George leans over her shoulder.

Like all the communications before, this one appears to be George's own message that has been returned. The sender shows up as 'System Administrator,' while 'Undeliverable Message' appears in the subject line. Embedded, after the nondelivery notice and a few lines of code, is the communication George supposedly sent, consisting of a few words and a Web link. At the judge's instruction, Dineesha clicks on the blue words. The site name, 'Death Watch,' in heavy black characters, springs onto the screen, accompanied by a line drawing of a wreath-covered coffin and a pointed inquiry: 'Have you ever asked yourself when you'll die? Or how?' A lengthy questionnaire follows, seeking age, health history, and occupational information, but George pages back to the message #1 somehow had directed to the judge's computer. It says, 'I know the answer.'

Beginning with his time as a State Defender after law school, George Mason has received his share of hate mail, which he has duly ignored. Criminal defendants, despite six eyewitnesses and security photos of them committing the stickup, have a notorious ability, after several months in the penitentiary, to explain to themselves that they would be free if they'd had a 'real' lawyer, instead of one receiving a paycheck from the same government that employed the prosecutor. The better-heeled crooks George represented in private practice also grew cantankerous sometimes, especially when they found that all the money they'd paid had merely paved the way to prison. In his current position, unhappy litigants occasionally vent too. None of these vitriolic communications has ever culminated in anything worse than a couple of manacled ex-clients, glowering at him across a courtroom, where they were appearing after a new arrest.

But the cool intelligence of #1's messages makes them more difficult to discount. They are unsigned, unlike most of the threatening correspondence George has received over the years, its erratic authors always eager for him to recall exactly whom he wronged. And, of course, recent events in Cincinnati, where a state court trial judge and his family were found murdered, have left everyone wearing a robe feeling more at risk.

The first returned message had simply said: 'You'll pay.' George had taken it as a mistake and apparently deleted it. But there was a second and a third with the same words within hours. George imagined they were spam. You'll pay—less. For car insurance. Mortgage payments. Viagra. Two days later, another followed: 'I said you'll pay. You will.' Since then there have been several more, each adding a new phrase making their meaning unambiguous. 'You'll pay. With blood.' And then: 'Your blood.' Then, 'You'll bleed.' At last, 'You'll die.' His permanent law clerk, John Banion, had just entered the judge's chambers when the message mentioning death popped up on George's screen, and he'd asked John to take a look. Banion appeared far more shaken than his boss and insisted on calling Court Security.

Court Security has arrived again now, in the person of its good-natured chief, Marina Giornale, who barrels into the reception area while George is still behind Dineesha. Less than five one, Marina makes up for size in energy. She issues greetings to the accompaniment of her raucous, rattling smoker's laugh and applies her usual robust hand-shake. She sports a black mullet, and no cosmetics. With the long khaki jacket that's part of her uniform and a wide black belt circumscribing her middle, she has the hefty look of a freezer in a packing crate.

"Is 'Death Watch' a real Web site?" the judge asks, as he shows her into his large private chambers. George closes both doors, one leading to the reception area, the other to the small adjoining office shared by his two law clerks.

"Oh, yeah. I was on the phone with the web-master all morning. He keeps telling me it's a free country." George Mason IV was one of the driving forces behind the Bill of Rights, and the judge often amuses himself by wondering how many hours it would take in today's America before his famous forebearer gave up on the First Amendment. There is no liberty that is not also the pathway to vice. The Internet has bred defiant communities of lunatics who once huddled in shamed isolation with their unsettling obsessions.

"So what did the Bureau say?" George asks when he's behind his large desk. Marina has taken a wooden armchair in front of him.

"They're going to run forensic software on your drive," she says, "when they get a chance, but they figure they have ninety-nine percent of what they'll find from capturing the e-mail headers."

"Which is?"

"Long short, there's no way to tell who's doing this."

"Great," George says.

"How much do you know about tracing e-mails, Your Honor?"

"Not a thing."

"Me neither," she says. "But I take good notes." With another hacking laugh, Marina fishes a small notebook from her jacket pocket. Marina is a cousin of the legendary and long dead Kindle County boss, Augustine Bolcarro. Nepotism being what it is, George had once assumed she was overmatched by her job. He was wrong. A former Kindle County police detective and the daughter of another dick, Marina has the crafty intuitions of somebody tutored over a lifetime. She has responded personally whenever he calls and, even more admirably, realized that her own staff, stretched thin by constant County budget cuts, will require assistance. She's involved the FBI, who are willing to help out since use of the interstate wires makes the threats to George a federal matter. Two silent technicians were in here for a day last week, imaging the judge's hard drive.

"The Bureau techies say that what we've got is a variation on something called a bounce-back attack, where somebody 'spoofs' "—she draws quotation marks in the air—"your e-mail address by placing it in the 'From' settings. Apparently, you could figure out how to do this with fifteen minutes of research. It's simple, as this kind of stuff goes, but it works.

"When the FBI examined the headers, it looked like all the messages come through an open mail server in the Philippines."

"'Open mail server'?"

She lifts a square hand. "An open mail relay server. Spammers set up most of them. Sometimes somebody muffs the security settings on their Web site, and everybody uses it until the owner catches on. But if the server is open, anyone can connect. It sends out any message given to it without checking who it's from. And open proxies don't usually keep logs of who routes through them either. The Bureau guys say this one may be related to a Web site hosted in China and owned by a company in London. I mean," says Marina, "good luck."

Disappointed, George looks around the room to think things over. One of the compensations of life on the appellate court is office space by the acre. His private chambers are nearly thirty feet by thirty, large enough to house all the knickknacks and mementos of his three decades in practice. The decorating, however, is strictly government-issue, an oceanic expanse of robin's egg carpeting and a lot of sturdy mahogany furniture manufactured by Prison Industries.

"Marina, this doesn't help your theory about Corazón, does it?" This name is why he closed the doors, and even so, he's dropped his voice. Mention of Corazón would intensify the alarm among his staff.

"Beg to differ, Judge. Gang Crimes is telling me

some of these Latin gangs are pretty with it. Lots of Internet identity theft. I'm not ruling Corazón out at all. Boys and girls at the Bureau like him too."

Based on the evidence so far, #1 could be anybody in the world with a computer and the judge's e-mail address. With little else to go on, Marina compiled a run of the cases George has sat on in the last three years. One name leapt out: Jaime Colon, known to everyone as 'El Corazón.' Corazón was the infamous Inca, or head, of Los Latinos Reyes, a street gang of several hundred members and a 'set' in the Almighty Latin Nation, the fastest growing of the Tri-Cities' three overarching gang organizations.

Decades ago, when George regularly visited the state penitentiary at Rudyard as a State Defender, he was routinely impressed that some inmates were regarded as so savage they frightened even the murderers and ruffians he was there to represent. That is Corazón—so evil, they say, that clocks stop and babies cry when he passes.

Little more than a year ago, the judge had written the opinion affirming Corazón's conviction for aggravated assault and obstruction of justice and, more to the point, his enhanced sentence of sixty years. Corazón had personally taken a tire iron to the girlfriend and two children, ages five and seven, of a jailed gang rival who was scheduled to testify against him in a drug case. Nor did Corazón's efforts at intimidation end there. When he was convicted, on the basis of a DNA match from fingernail scrapings taken at the hospital from the victims, who were prudent enough to flee to Mexico before the trial, Corazón promised to wreak revenge on the trial judge, the prosecutors, the cops, and anybody else who had a hand in sending him away.

As a result, Corazón is now held in the state's lone supermax facility, his cell an eight-by-eight concrete block where he enjoys extemporaneous communications with no one except the guards and his mother, with whom he gets a single monitored visit each month. Nonetheless, Corazón's sheer badness has made him the prime suspect. The intrigue of organizing the intimidation of a judge while being held incommunicado is a challenge he'd welcome, especially since he could take it on with little fear of the consequences. A longer sentence is meaningless to a man of forty-two. If he's caught, his principal punishment will be a period of receiving a tasteless hash called meal loaf instead of real food.

"Bureau agents paid him a visit last week," Marina says. "Corazón loves to get out and shoot the breeze, doesn't even bother with his lawyer. The Feebies were asking him about a couple kids in his outfit doing dirt time," she says, meaning that the gang members were murdered, "but they worked your name in."

"And?"

"He didn't twitch. Still, they wanted him to know they had his scent."

When it comes to solving crimes, the obvious answer is usually the right one—the jealous husband is the murderer of his ex, the fired employee is the one who sabotaged the pipes at the factory—but the judge remains skeptical that a man who used a tire iron to silence witnesses would bother with something this cagey.

"I'm not sold on Corazón, Marina. Frankly, I still think whoever's doing this is just talking dirty." The paranoid crackpots are the correspondents George has learned to fear—they attack thinking they're protecting themselves. But a rational person intent on mayhem does not send warnings, simply because they'd make reprisals harder to carry out. George is convinced that #1's only aim is to roil his peace of mind, a goal far too civilized for Corazón.

"I take this creep seriously, Judge."

Inclined to debate, George chooses not to answer. He's long understood that people in law enforcement yearn to see themselves as knight protectors—you could bet a goodly sum, for example, that Marina Giornale had grown up reading everything she could about St. Joan. The more gravely Marina takes these messages, the more important they make her.

"And the Bureau and my people agree on one thing," she says.

"Which is?"

"It's time for a detail."

"No," says George, as he has said before to the idea of a security detail. A bodyguard would be an infernal nuisance—and far worse, something that couldn't be hidden from Patrice. He has said nothing to his wife about these threats, and he does not intend to. Her own condition provides enough worry at the moment. "I can't handle that at home, Marina."

Aware of Patrice's illness, Marina offers a lingering sympathetic look before massaging her jaw to contemplate.

"Look, Judge, how about this? Your house is your house. I can't tell you what to do there. You're not listed, right?"

An unlisted phone has been required since George's days as a defense lawyer, the better to avoid the 3:00 A.M. call from the white-collar client who'd just awoken from a nightmare of prison.

"But when you get to County property, Judge, you're on my turf. So all due respect and genuflecting several times, and doing the dance of the seven veils"—she smiles in her apple-cheeked way, a winning child—"I still gotta have somebody with you. When I run through the God-forbids in my head, Your Honor, I can't even imagine how I'd explain leaving you uncovered."

She is saying that he can't require her to engage in the law enforcement equivalent of malpractice. He slaps his thighs in resignation, and Marina quickly offers her hand.

George sees her out. As he opens the door, Banion is there, a draft opinion in hand that has just arrived from another judge's chambers. On the threshold, Marina turns back to both of them.

"Say, you drew quite a crowd this morning." She's referring to the horde trying to gain admission to the oral argument in *Warnovits*, which her staff was required to handle.

Recalled, the case immediately nags at the judge. It's like a bad meal, a fight with your spouse, something carried with you that douses your mood all day.

"I hate that case," he responds. This is no news to Banion. The judge assigned John to review the portions of the videotape that Sapperstein said should not have been shown to the jury after George reached the point where he could not stand watching any more. Ever impassive, John shows little more than a mild frown. But Marina draws back.

"Why's that? I thought deciding the big ones is what you guys live for."

She's right about that. In fact, it's part of the larger riddle about his reactions to the case. George wanted to be a judge because the job matters, because you are trusted to be the conscience of your community and to apply the time-ennobled traditions of the law. He often feels the weight of those responsibilities, yet seldom regrets them. But now he gives his head a decorous shake, pretending that propriety rather than utter mystification prevents him from trying to explain.

3

HOSPITAL CALL

George races down the judges' private corridor toward the conference chambers adjacent to the appellate courtroom. He is actually a few minutes ahead of schedule for his meeting with Purfoyle and Koll, but he wants to phone Patrice, and he stops by a long window where cell reception is better. It is a goofy rectitude, he knows, uncomfortably reminiscent of his father, to avoid personal calls from the County line in his chambers, but as a judge he never shakes the expectation that he must lead by example in matters large and small. He wears a suit and tie each day and requires similar apparel of his staff, notwithstanding the more casual attire favored by his colleagues when they do not have to appear in the courtroom. He is determined that, if nothing else, he will always look the part: tall, trim, gray-haired, and handsome in a conventional middle-aged way. Standard-issue white guy.

"Fine. Tired. Not a bad day at all," Patrice says when he reaches her at the hospital. He has tried her several times this morning, but the line has been constantly engaged. At the moment, Patrice's interaction with the human race is confined to the telephone. "They think my Geiger levels may be down enough tonight to let you in the room. Most women want a man's heart, Georgie. I bet you were never counting on risking your thyroid."

"Gladly, mate," he answers, a term of mutual endearment. "Any organ you like." The Masons have always relished each other's company and the way they generally ride along on a current of low-voltage humor. But at the moment, his druthers are to be more sincere. To many men George knows, marriage is a war against their longings. Yet he is among the happy few. For more than thirty years now, he has been able to say that he has wanted no one more than Patrice.

These sentiments swamp him frequently these days. The nodule on Patrice's thyroid was discovered on February 10, and when he stood in a store a day later reading the humid poetry on several valentines, he actually wept. But at the moment he feels obliged to keep this torrent of affection to himself. For Patrice right now the only acceptable behavior is what she deems 'normal'—no dramatics and certainly no proclamations of a kind that Patrice, being Patrice, would deride as 'soft and runny.'

"How about if I bring dinner?" George asks. "We can eat together. Any cravings?"

"No more limp green beans. Something with spice."

"Mexican?"

"Perfect. After eight. That'll be thirty-six hours. But they won't let you stay long, mate."

Yesterday at 6:00 A.M., he'd brought Patrice to West Bank Lutheran–Sinai. There she'd swallowed a large white pill full of iodine-131. Now she may not have any physical contact with other human beings. The radiation broiling through her and

41

eradicating every thyroid cell, especially the way-
ward ones that have wandered dangerously into
other portions of her body, might also kill the
healthy gland in someone else. The treatment has a
long record of success, but it is disquieting to
experience. At the moment, Patrice would be less
isolated on a lepers' island, where at least she would
have company. At West Bank, she is housed alone
in a small, white room of cinder block laid over a
lining of lead. The decorating aims to avoid the
sterile appearance of a hospital room, with the result
that the space instead has the dismal look of a cheap
motel, with scarred furniture and a thin chenille
spread on the bed. Any item that will exit the area
must be destroyed by special staff or quarantined—
the books and magazines Patrice has been reading,
her undergarments, and the leavings in the bedpan
she must use. Her pulse and temperature are monitored electronically, and the orderlies serve her
meals through a lead flap in the door.

Yesterday, even George was not permitted in her
room. Instead, his wife and he spoke through telephone handsets on either side of a large window cut
into the wall adjoining her bed, on which Patrice

can raise the shade. For George, the comparison with his professional life was unavoidable. How many clients in how many institutions had he conversed with this way? And how many of their fellow inmates had he surreptitiously eyed with the usual mix of empathy and judgment, as the prisoners pawed the glass or wept, with a child or lover on the other side, feeling only now the sharpest tooth of confinement, and thus of crime? With his own wife isolated this way, George could not shake a miserable, low conviction that he had failed. Their conversation was listless and unsettled. The glass between them might well have been her illness. After thirty-three years, it has turned out that their life together is a matter of grace rather than mutual will. Patrice is sick and he is not. 'There is really no such thing,' one social worker warned a support group for spouses, 'as having cancer together.'

"Didn't you have arguments this morning?" Patrice asks. "How were they?"

"Lackluster in most cases. But we just heard *Warnovits*. The high school rape case?"

"The one on the news? Were the attorneys good?"

"Not especially, but I was sitting with Nathan Koll, who planted a roadside bomb for the lawyers. Now I've got to go to conference and watch him wrap his arms around himself so he can pat his own back. I'm due now."

"Then go ahead, George. I'll call if I fail the Geiger counter."

Clicking off, he peers from the window into the canyon of U.S. 843 that separates the Central Branch Courthouse from the Center City, and beyond that to the downtown towers, stolid monuments to capital. Summer is coming, a season of ripeness and promise, but the feeling in his own soul remains autumnal. George is off his stride and knows it. Revered as calm and poised, he is lately more likely to become unsettled, as he has been by *Warnovits*. He has occasionally turned snappish with his staff and has grown uncharacteristically absentminded. About ten days ago, he lost his cell phone—who knows where? He noticed it was gone on his way back from a Bar Association luncheon he'd attended with several of his colleagues. He had Dineesha ransack his chambers while his clerks called all over the Center City. For the moment, he is using Patrice's spare.

Some might think that it is #1 getting on his nerves. That probably hasn't helped, but this moodiness predates the first e-mail George received from his anonymous tormentor. Instead his unease correlates more clearly with the time of Patrice's diagnosis. He is convinced in every fiber that his wife is not going to die. The doctors have done everything short of issue guarantees. Her chances approach nineteen in twenty, and even those odds take no account of the robust good health in which she otherwise remains—lean, athletic, tanned, still beautiful.

Yet as George's friend Harrison Oakey has put it, serious illness at this age is like the lights flashing in the theater lobby. If life is a three-act play, then the curtain has gone up on the finale. After John Banion had read #1's message saying 'You'll die,' the judge had tried to settle his clerk with humor while they awaited Marina. 'This guy has no future in journalism,' George told him, 'because that's not breaking news.'

45

Still, irony gets you only so far. The facts settle hard. And with them comes an inevitable calculation of pluses and minuses. George tends to be unsparing, even harsh, in his self-assessments. Husband. Father. Lawyer. Judge. These days, he seems to be keeping a cool eye on the scoreboard.

4

THE CONFERENCE

Nathan Koll is a formidable, if ponderous, intellect with the academic equivalent of a five-star general's chestful of medals: first in every class with Latinate honors, Order of the Coif, law review, blah blah blah. Real fucking smart. George always wonders how Koll sees himself. Probably as lawyers are in the ideal, a tower of icy reason. But Nathan is in fact as eccentric as a street person. For one thing, he does not bathe. Inhaling the body odor is like dragging a tree saw through your nose. Sharing the tiny robing room with him, where the judges don their long black gowns before arguments, is a much-lamented ordeal. His fingernails are grimy, and his wavy black hair is pasted to his forehead.

George has long viewed Nathan's unwillingness to surrender even to soap and water as a function of his noticeable paranoid streak, in which the man's fierce commitment to winning every argument may be a way to prove to himself that he is safe from everyone. Not that Nathan would ever admit to a personal stake. He never says, 'I want,' 'I believe,' 'I need,' nor will he acknowledge that anybody else might have any pride or attachment to his position. Everything is presented merely as a matter of ruthless logic, often with the traces of a snigger betraying itself at the corners of his lips.

Off the bench, Koll keeps himself remote as a survivalist and refuses to give anyone, even his own staff, either his home address or phone. He can be reached only by BlackBerry. He has a wife, a beaten-down-looking Asian woman. George has met her twice but has yet to hear her speak.

Nathan sits by interim appointment of the state Supreme Court, filling the remaining term in a seat being cut for budgetary reasons after 2008. He accepted the job sure it would propel him to the U.S. Court of Appeals in Chicago after John Kerry's election. Given present realities, Nathan would like to retain this position indefinitely, but there's little chance of that. No vacancies are anticipated for years on the court. More to the point, Koll would find a complete absence of support among the judges, whom he has irritated to a person, George included. Judge Mason no longer cares that Koll and he often end up on the same side of issues or that Koll is a uniquely able ally, artful in using cost-benefit analysis to the detriment of conservatives, who tend to respond as if he has broken into their toolshed. Nathan regards himself as the uninhibited protector of the oppressed, but this is so small a portion of the bizarre parade that is his everyday performance on the bench that it is a virtual lie by omission.

Now George braces himself as he enters the conference chambers beside the appellate court-room. Like everything else in the old courthouse, the room has a classical finish and looks a bit like a private dining room in a men's club, right down to the baubled chandelier. To protect the privacy of these deliberations, there are no windows, and even the law clerks who will do the first drafts of the opinions are excluded so the judges may speak freely, without the need to save face in the presence of juniors.

The other member of the morning panel, Summerset Purfoyle, is seated with Nathan at the Chippendale conference table, long enough to allow all twenty members of the appellate court to confer in the rare case when they sit together en banc. With Koll here, Summer has taken a chair a good ten feet away, and George follows suit on the opposite side.

As the senior judge on the panel, George presides and calls the cases for discussion in the order they were heard this morning. Usually the work of the court is divided evenly between civil and criminal matters and, more pointedly, justice at the American extremes, for the very rich and for the very poor. As a rule, civil appeals make sense only when the financial or personal stakes are high, because the appellant has to post a bond guaranteeing that the trial court winner will be paid, then foot the bill for an attorney to comb the record looking for mistakes.

On the criminal side, the matters reflect the reali-ties of the courtrooms downstairs, where the defendants are overwhelmingly poor young males, represented by state-paid counsel. In nine cases out of ten, the decision of the appellate court will be the last real chance for men sentenced to significant prison terms. The state Supreme Court rarely grants further review in criminal matters. George's job is not to rejudge these cases for the jury. But he takes with a solemnity approaching religious commitment his obligation to be able to say, all things considered, that the defendant was convicted fairly.

The three judges move through the civil cases argued in advance of *Warnovits* without much debate. The first two, a child custody dispute and a fight over air rights between two corporations, are affirmances; the third, a $9 million personal-injury verdict against a furnace manufacturer, must be set aside because the trial judge, a lunkhead named Myron Spiro, whom the appellate court often reverses, disallowed a lawful defense. As presiding judge, George has the right to decide who will author the court's opinions in these cases, but his practice is to await volunteers, and Nathan, predictably, says he's willing to do all three. Koll writes like the wind, seldom needing much help from his clerks, and it is sometimes an irresistible temptation to let him do most of the work. But Summer wants the custody case, and Nathan defers on that, taking the other two. Privately, George is delighted that Koll will handle the reversal of the furnace verdict, because Nathan will not resist subjecting Spiro to the ridicule he deserves.

"All right," says George. "Let's earn the big bucks. *Warnovits*."

As the presiding judge, George has the right to speak first, but he remains mysteriously confused and heavyhearted about the matter. Instead, he turns to Koll.

"Nathan, I need to hear more about this business you brought up at the end of the oral argument concerning the state eavesdropping statute."

In truth, George knows all he needs to, because the motives were plain. Koll, ever-victorious, had figured out a way to demonstrate to the packed courtroom, including the full row of press, that the celebrated Jordan Sapperstein had overlooked a winning argument.

An added victim of this display was the time-ravaged warhorse who had followed Sapperstein to the podium to argue for the state, Tommy Molto. The judges of the Kindle County Superior Court recently appointed Tommy the County's acting Prosecuting Attorney, making him the second successor to the unexpired term of the elected P.A. Muriel Wynn, who had barely warmed the chair before mounting a successful campaign for state Attorney General. The first interim P.A., Horace Donnelly, had resigned after about four months, when the *Tribune* discovered that he had left markers on the state's riverboat casinos that totaled twice his annual salary. Molto was the safe choice, a relentless and unforgiving career prosecutor who by now seems destined to die of elevated blood pressure in the midst of some courtroom harangue about the miserable shortcomings of a defendant.

Today, Tommy was making a point by his presence, showing that the P.A.'s office gave *Warnovits* premium significance. In truth, George views Molto as a better appellate advocate than many of his deputies. He gets to the point, answers questions directly, and does his best with his argument's weaknesses without pretending that doubts are unreasonable. Representing the state in *Warnovits*, Molto meandered safely through his response, first explaining how the case comfortably fit within the legislative exceptions to the state statute of limitations. Then he echoed the points Koll had made in disputing Sapperstein's claim that the videotape of the rape should have been severely edited before being shown to the jury.

Not uncharacteristically, Koll suddenly seemed to abandon his own point of view.

'Mr. Molto,' he said, 'after this Court's decision in *Brewer*, can you and I agree that the videotaping of Mindy DeBoyer without her consent violated the state's eavesdropping law?'

Brewer, decided a few months ago, concerned a junior high school janitor who had used the camera on his cell phone to collect images in the boys' locker room. Molto nodded cautiously. The weight of every crime and every bad guy who had slipped away seemed to have led to an overall descent in his ruined face, and what little of the gray hair that remained atop his head stood straight up in an unfortunate breeze from the courthouse ventilation system. His suit, as usual, looked as if it had been stuffed into his desk drawer for storage overnight.

'I agree, but that crime was not charged, Your Honor.'

'Indeed, Mr. Molto. That crime was not charged. And Section (c)(6) of the eavesdropping law says clearly, and I quote, "Evidence obtained in violation of this chapter is inadmissible in any civil or criminal case, except a prosecution for violation of this chapter." That to me means that your videotape clearly should not have been received in evidence.'

Molto looked as if he'd been stabbed. Behind him at the defendants' table, Sapperstein rocketed back against his chair so hard that he might have done with an air bag.

"You're not suggesting, Nate, are you," says Summerset Purfoyle now, "that we should reverse these convictions on that basis?"

"Why not? No tape, no case."

"But Sapperstein didn't argue the point here, and neither did the defense lawyers at trial. We

SCOTT TUROW

can't take it up now." It is the essential nature of an appeal that it is decided in a kind of twilight zone—only what was recorded in the trial court can be considered. The whole truth—the contents of the police reports, the statements of witnesses not called, the byplay between the lawyers and the judge at sidebars or in chambers—may not be taken into account. It is like writing a history from the fragments left after a fire. In the same vein, it is a cardinal rule that legal objections that the trial judge had no chance to correct cannot be raised on appeal.

"Foolish on his part," answers Koll. "Damn near malpractice." The truth, George realizes; is that until *Brewer*, a few months ago, even the best lawyer might not have thought that a law passed in the 1970s to safeguard the conversations of citizens—and legislators—from unwanted snooping was worded broadly enough to reach video recording as well.

"Nathan, that provision was meant to keep people who eavesdrop from taking advantage of their crime in court," Summer says. "A fellow can't bug his wife, then use the tapes in their divorce case.

But I just don't see the sense, in circumstances like these, of saying that the defendants can't be prosecuted for anything but illegal surveillance, no matter how god-awful the conduct that's recorded there. Why would the legislature want to short-change the victim like that?"

"The words of the statute couldn't be clearer. It's plain error," Koll adds, invoking the doctrine that allows the appellate court to recognize overlooked trial mistakes when they would clearly alter the outcome.

George reacts to this. "It has to be more than plain error, Nathan. We're referees, not players. We can't advance our own arguments, unless ignoring them leads to a miscarriage of justice. That's the standard we have to apply."

"And how is it not a miscarriage of justice to convict four men when the whole case against them is inadmissible?"

George is somewhat surprised that Koll is so wedded to his argument. Often, he musters these arid academic displays to impress or belittle, then leaves them in the courtroom.

Summerset continues shaking his head. He was

a famous soul singer who went to law school between tours, one night quarter at a time, so that he could manage his own career. When his star sank to the point that he was appearing only at outdoor summer festivals and high school reunions, he decided to capitalize on his remaining name recognition by running for judge in the hope of achieving a reliable income. The bar associations wrung their hands over a judicial candidate who sang one of his two big hits, 'Made a Man for a Woman' and 'Hurtin' Heart,' at every campaign stop, but Summer's performance on the bench has been solid. His elevation to the appellate court was a way to get him out of the one job he didn't belong in—he was a poor manager as Presiding Judge of the torts trial division in the Superior Court. Here he is neither George's most distinguished colleague nor his least. He continues to work hard and shows uncommon common sense, rendering sound, pragmatic interpretations of the law.

And the view he expresses several times now is that convicting these young men is far from unjust. Race, the perpetual theme song of American life, might be a factor in his evaluation, but George, who has sat with Purfoyle dozens of times, doubts that. Summer, much like George himself, usually sides with the prosecutors, except in clear cases of police misbehavior. Nathan duels with Summerset for some time, trying to nudge the facts with little hypothetical alterations into a shape allowing him to prevail, but increasingly he casts his dark, squinty look toward George, who obviously holds the deciding vote.

The person on the street might think judges are emperors who wave their scepters and do what they like, but in George's experience, all of them attempt to apply the law. Words are sometimes as elusive as fish, and reasonable minds often differ on the meaning of cases and statutes, but it is still the actual language that has to guide a judge. George concentrates on the question: Is convicting these boys on the basis of a videotape that should not have been admitted 'a miscarriage of justice'?

Incongruously, it is the tape itself that stands out in his mind as he endeavors to answer. Sapperstein's arguments required George to view the video, locked in his inner chambers. Hard to shock when it comes to crime, George could stomach only a portion of it before assigning Banion to go through it frame by frame and produce a sterile description.

But the ten minutes or so George took in still reverberate. Mindy DeBoyer was a deadweight throughout, her limbs like wet laundry. The teased ribbons of her dark hair were conveniently pushed across her face, while her naked hips and one leg straddled the arm of a Chesterfield chair, as if the fully dressed upper body slumped on the cushion below—the head, the heart—did not exist. It was crime at its purest, in which empathy, that most fundamental aspect of human morality, evaporated and another being became only a target for untamed fantasy. The sexual acts were committed in emphatic plunging motions of pure aggression, and the way the boys exposed themselves to one another before and after, amid much wild hooting, could only be labeled depraved—not in any puritanical sense but because George sensed that these young men were dominated by impulses they would ordinarily have rejected. But if the purpose of the criminal law is to state emphatically that some behavior is beyond toleration, then this case surely requires that declaration.

"I'm afraid that I'm going to have to side with Summerset on this one," he says. Koll makes a face. "Nathan, the defendants are entitled to be judged on what they argued, not what they didn't. I will say, though, that Sapperstein's claim about the statute of limitations has quite a bit of traction with me. Ms. DeBoyer knew she might have been raped but said nothing. How can we say the crime was concealed?"

"Because that was the trial judge's conclusion," answers Summer at once. "He saw the young woman testify. He felt that, given her age and inexperience, those boys kept her from knowing enough to report the crime. We have to defer to him."

In George's mind Sapperstein has made his most telling argument on this point, contending that the trial judge's reliance on Mindy's age means he was essentially applying an exception to the statute of limitations for crimes committed against minors. In such a case, the victim has a year from her eighteenth birthday to report the offense. But Mindy was three months past nineteen when the tape came to light.

Much as Koll turned to him a moment before, George now looks at Nathan.

"I'm afraid that I'm going to have to side with Summerset on this one," Koll answers, echoing George's precise words. Tit for tat. So much for the majesty of the law.

George ponders where they are. Three judges and three different opinions in a case that is already highly controversial. As the senior, George is supposed to fashion a compromise that will not lead the court into ridicule. A reversal, with no agreement why, will only fan the flames in Glen Brae. More important, their job is to declare the law, not hold up their palms and say to the world 'Who knows?' Accordingly, he decides to write the opinion himself. Years ago, before Rusty Sabich became Chief Judge, when the appellate court was a retirement camp for able party loyalists, opinions were assigned in advance by rotation, and dissents were all but forbidden. In practice, appeals were argued to a court of one, with the lawyers standing at the podium engaged in a legal shell game, attempting to guess which of the three judges was actually deciding the case.

"I'll take this one," he says, and with that stands, calling the conference to a close.

Nettled as always when he does not get his way, Koll directs a heavy look at George.

"And are we affirming or reversing?"

"Well, Nathan, you'll have to read my draft. I'll circulate it within the week." Koll will write his own opinion anyway, a concurrence or a dissent, depending on which way George goes. "This case is—" says Judge Mason and stops cold. He still has no idea how he is going to vote, which argument he'll champion and which he'll reject. Decisiveness is a job requirement and one at which he normally excels. His continuing discomfort with *People v. Warnovits* remains troubling but suddenly not as much as what he was on the verge of blurting out. He has no clue even what the words could mean, but he was ready to tell his two colleagues, 'This case is me.'

5

THE GARAGE

In the late 1980s, the Third District Appellate Court
was relocated by the County Board. Litigation had
become a growth business in Kindle County, much
like everywhere else in America, and the need for
more civil courtrooms in the Superior Court building, known as the Temple, had forced the appellate
judges to take up residence a mile away in the
Central Branch Courthouse, where criminal cases
were tried. Bolstered by Reagan-era law enforcement money, the County constructed a large criminal court annex. The appellate judges were allotted

most of the grand spaces in the old building, which had been erected with the rich architectural detail characteristic of public projects during the Depression, when skilled tradesmen worked cheap. Nonetheless, many of the jurists were unhappy to move out of Center City. Beyond U.S. 843, the area is blighted, sometimes dangerous, and offers few decent spots for lunch. But George Mason, who began his professional career in this courthouse as a Deputy State Defender, relishes every day the fact that he has come full circle.

Now, in the adjacent concrete parking structure, Judge Mason throws his briefcase down on the front seat of his car. He triggers the ignition so he can put on the air—it is another close evening in early June—but he has no intention of driving anywhere yet. The 1994 Lexus LS 400 is a remaining prize of his flush times in private practice, and he maintains the car devotedly, in part because it is the only space in the world he thinks of as exclusively his. Here at the end of the day, he often reflects on cases and personal issues, when he is finally free from the robe, whose weight he feels everywhere in the court-house, whether he is wearing it or not.

The gloomy parking garage would not strike many as a welcoming spot for reflection, especially since the Central Branch Courthouse is where many of the County's most dangerous citizens must report monthly while they are out on bail. Although the garage is heavily patrolled by Marina's forces during business hours, perpetual budget cuts have left only a small crew on duty after 6:00 P.M., when George customarily returns. Through the years, the garage has been the scene of stickups, beatings, and more than one shooting, involving Kindle County's eternally warring gangs, the Black Saints Disciples, the Gangster Outlaws, and the Almighty Latin Nation, and their constituent 'sets.' 'Get in and get out' is the standard advice.

At the moment, the judge has his eye on two kids, one long, one short, both in sweatshirts, who have popped up in his rear- and side-view mirrors several times. From their looks, he takes it that the two are probably here for late-afternoon drug court. At one point, he feared they were actually circling him, but they disappeared soon afterward. Either way, he is not about to move. The vague tingle of lurking danger has always been one of the attractions of the garage for George, whose entire professional life has been founded on the conviction that he knows himself best under these shadows.

The driver's seat in this car is as large and soft as a piece of den furniture, and he motors it back from the wheel, reclining slightly, so he can ask himself the question that has waited for hours. What is it that lingers with him about *People v. Warnovits*? 'This case is me,' he almost declared to his colleagues several hours before. *Me?* He had meant to say 'my,' on his way to offering, as a good-natured jest, 'This case is *my* problem.' Even that remark seems oddly proprietary in retrospect, since his role in the ideal is to speak for all three judges.

And so the inner tuning fork has been struck. He continues, eyes closed meditatively, trolling his memory until what he has long sought is suddenly snagged. His grin with the first recollection fades as the problem becomes apparent.

The event took place more than forty years ago, in a different world. In Charlottesville in those days, no one would have found it humorous to hear him say as a first-year—never 'freshman'—that he was there to become a gentleman and a scholar. He attended class in a sport coat and tie. Like all the men in his family, he was colorblind. His mother had given him an index card explaining how to match his clothes, but he misplaced it and stepped out of the old dorm each morning expecting to be greeted with smirks.

He had not been happy then. The chafing and boiling that would ultimately drive him here, a thousand miles from home, had started. He could not have named everything that bothered him—his mother's relentless social pretensions, his father's rigid adherence to faith and honor as the credo of a Southern gentleman—but coming of age amid the unyielding proprieties of southern Virginia, where there were few open questions, whether about God or Yankees or Negroes, felt like growing up in a lightless closet. By high school, he was determined to escape and read Kerouac, Burroughs, Ginsberg, bards of the liberation that he believed in as a matter of spirit but that he had no idea how to practice.

Which was why it mattered so much to him that he was a virgin. He was supposed to be, of course, if you had asked his minister or his teachers or his parents. It was 1964. But both body and soul yearned for freedom.

Six weeks into his initial term, the college had its first party weekend. Having forsaken his high school girlfriend, a pretty but narrow young woman, he watched with envy as other hometown girls arrived on campus. George was miserable and alone. The reliable bond of male affection that had been forged in those first weeks was broken now by the preeminent claim exerted by the other half of the species.

As recompense for abandoning their double, George's roommate had bought him a cheap bottle of Scotch. Alcohol was one of the grave sins condemned in his home that he had been quickest to take up, and George was soon drunk on hard liquor for the first time in his life. By now it was nearly 10:00 P.M. The couples had finished their restaurant dinners, danced in the sweaty mash of fraternity parties, and were retreating to the dorm for the moments that mattered most to many of these young men, before parietal hours ended and the women had to return to the local rooming houses or the dorms at a nearby female college where they had been put up. With the Scotch under his arm, George careered through the halls. The doors to most of the rooms were cracked open an inch or two in accord with university rules, allowing tracks from *Meet the Beatles!* to scream out from the hi-fis within. Knowing that men and women were in each other's arms, necking, groping, running the bases, George was battered with longing.

In that condition, he ran into his best friend, Mario Alfieri. Mario had come here from Queens on a wrestling scholarship and seemed as out of place in genteel Charlottesville as a platypus. Boisterous, profane, wisecracking, he was the renegade George wanted to be, and they had developed a quick appreciation for each other. Coming downstairs, carrying a bucket of ice, Mario grabbed George's elbow.

'You won't believe this,' he said, repeating it several times as he bent with laughter. 'Brierly's got a girl up in the second-floor hallway pulling a train.'

George knew the term, but still he looked at Mario without comprehension.

'No lie,' Mario said. 'She's out in a refrigerator box, entertaining the troops. So, Georgie boy, listen to me. You're saved. Saved.' Mario knew George's barren sexual history. 'Get yourself up there.'

'Did you go?'

'I have a date, knucklehead.' George had met the young woman briefly. She was the sister of another wrestler whom Mario had been persuaded to invite blind on the promise that she was as irreverent as he was. In person, Joan had proved even prettier than her snapshot, but she was also one of those rare women who seemed defiant even standing still. 'Five to one, I get nothing off her,' Mario had whispered to George.

'What about the syph?' George asked now, contemplating what supposedly was occurring upstairs.

'What about getting laid?' Mario reached back to his wallet and slapped the emergency prophylactic always there into George's hand. 'Greater love,' Mario said. He pushed his friend to the staircase with both hands.

Coming off the landing, George found a scene that seemed entirely improbable, notwithstanding Mario's description. A huge carton, about eight feet long and four feet high, had been wedged across the threshold of Hugh Brierly's room at the far end of the hall. Projecting between the open flaps on one side, George saw a white shirttail and four naked legs, two with pairs of men's trousers and boxer shorts bunched at the ankles. The boy was on his toes while the box lurched minutely with his efforts.

At least two dozen men were lined up on either side of the hallway to witness this, all with their ties loosened and drinks in hand. They jolted in laughter and slapped one another's shoulders, shouting out lewd one-liners. But none of them, no matter what, took his eyes off the box. It was as if it contained the secret of fire. Every now and then, one or two would break away to peer into the open end of the carton and shout obscene encouragement to the fellow inside.

George crept closer until he realized that he'd chosen the side of the hall where the line had formed. The nearer he came to the front, the more he felt the frantic charge that seemed to grip all of the spectators. A dull knocking sounded from the box, and at one point as George waited, a boy inside suddenly screamed 'Score!' The men in the corridor erupted in laughter that seemed wild enough to loosen the bricks of the building.

In front of him in line was Tom McMillan, another first-year. 'I'm going again,' he told George. The girl, McMillan explained, had appeared at the football game alone, apparently ditched by her date. She had started talking to Brierly and Goren, two boys from the dorm, both dateless too, and returned here with them. The three drank for hours, until they were all witless from the favored libation of the weekend, a cocktail of grain alcohol and fruit punch consumed directly from a Hi-C can. At some point, the girl had said that she'd be everybody's date, and that had become a motif for their increasingly lewd conversation, until the boys began to press the idea that she could not disappoint them. Brierly had found this refrigerator box, and the girl had supposedly climbed in with him, laughing.

As George neared the head of the line, a first-year named Rogers Peterson came charging down the hall toward Brierly.

'Jesus,' he said. 'Jesus. Some of us have our dates

up here. We can't have this going on. What's wrong with all of you? What should we tell our girls?'

'Tell them not to look,' Brierly said, and the mob howled, jeering Peterson as he retreated.

The throng of onlookers was growing fast. Word was spreading. Fellows in ties and blazers had actually stepped out on their dates for a few minutes and come running. George could feel his anxieties wearing through the effects of the Scotch, and he noticed that there were far more men watching than awaiting a turn. But the line was growing behind him fast enough that he knew there was no time for indecision.

When McMillan reached the head, Brierly waved him away.

'No seconds, not yet.'

McMillan was still protesting when a short, obese fellow George did not know backed out of the box, refastening his trousers.

'What a swamp!' he said, and the hallway again rocked with laughter.

Brierly pointed at George. 'Next,' he said, 'in the tunnel of love.' Only then did George see that Hugh was collecting money, 'Rent,' Brierly said. 'It's my box.'

George dumbly picked ten dollars, a week's spending money, out of his wallet.

'You have five minutes, Mason. Do your best.'

He did not even touch his belt to lower his trousers until he had crept inside, where he was overwhelmed by the intense odor. Someone, probably the girl, had vomited, and the smell was heavy in the close air, which was sodden with overheated breaths and perspiration. The box was so low he could not really kneel over her and had to support himself with one hand to pull down his pants. The girl was talking to herself, half sentences, song lyrics, he thought, a high-pitched mumbo jumbo. He made out one phrase she sang: 'I want to hold your hand.'

She addressed him when he touched her. 'Hey, honey,' she said in a lyrical, drunken, carefree voice, seeming to relish this fleeting moment of anesthesia.

He wanted to make the most of his opportunity and explored the girl's skinny body without much tenderness. A wool skirt was in a lump at her waist, and a silky undergarment had been pushed up to her shoulders. Lying down, she had only the smallest swell of breasts and tiny nipples like peas.

When he had first crawled into the carton, revolted by the heat and the smells, it occurred to him that he had to do no more than push his pants down to his ankles. None of the boys in the hallway would know what had happened. He could rock a bit, then talk the good game that so many fools talked on Sunday morning. But that was the point. No one would know. He was free. And although he was drilled by terror, he was going ahead, because he wanted to get this moment over with. There were two groups in the world, the ones who had and the ones who hadn't, and he was convinced that every uncertainty of his age would be abated if he crossed that divide.

When he entered her, after a terrible moment of fumbling, his body was divided by a scream from his own heart. With startling clarity, he heard warnings of damnation. But those were the voices he was determined to be free from, and so he continued and finished that way, determined, somehow isolated from the sensations of pleasure. The girl, as he remembered, had rested a hand on his back and made some effort to move below him.

When he was done, he refastened his trousers.

'Are you okay?' he whispered before he crawled out.

'Oh, honey,' she answered.

'No, really. Are you okay?' He touched her cheek for the first time.

She was singing again, with a sudden clarity that frightened him.

His eyes stung when he emerged into the blazing fluorescence of the hallway. A few men reached out to pat his back and joked about his speed—he might not have been inside two minutes—but he wanted to escape the hungry pack. They had no idea what had actually happened. It was not what they thought or what they were celebrating. A moment later he was downstairs, trying to make whatever he could out of having passed through the membrane between his fantasies and his life. The Scotch was starting to back up on him.

Mario Alfieri's blind date, Joan—with whom Mario was destined to spend the next thirty-seven years, until he died in the second World Trade Center tower on 9/11—appeared from the door of the bath designated for the weekend as the ladies' room. She nearly ran into George while he was still trying to jam his shirttails into his trousers.

'What happened to you?' she asked.

He could not find a discreet answer. 'Life is strange,' he told her.

As much of a wise guy as Mario, Joan eyed him at length and asked, 'Compared to what?'

Over the decades, when Judge Mason has loitered with the incident in recollection—and that is not often—he has dismissed it under the rubric of amusing follies of youth. Everyone had a first experience, and half of them were crazy. Faltering. Unsuccessful. Life and love moved forward to a better footing. He has not fully considered this moment in years and never attached to it the name he is required to apply today: a crime.

He reconsiders the word, the idea. *Crime?* He is a lawyer, a master of distinctions. It is not the same at all. Yet the incident is too close to the case he heard this morning for any comfort. The girl was drunk. Virtually incoherent. Her actions might have passed for consent in those days. But not now. The men in that dormitory hallway, including most especially him, had, in every sense of the antique phrase, taken advantage of her.

In the tomb darkness of the parking garage, George Mason feels how harshly his heart is beating. This is serious. Because he realizes that he has suddenly lost one of the comforts of middle age. There is joint pain, fading hearing, and trouble recalling names—even cancer. But generally speaking, not this. Yet now his soul seems as insubstantial as a fume. At the age of fifty-nine, George Mason wonders who he is.

6

PATRICE

Did we ever talk about my first time?" George asks Patrice at the hospital that night. The radioactive treatment required her to suspend her thyroid-replacement therapy, and she has been left feeling, as she puts it, 'energetic as moss.' At 7:00 P.M., she lies in the hospital bed, paging through a magazine. George himself is wrapped like a present—paper gown, cap, and booties—and sits behind a line taped on the floor, seven yards from his wife. Tonight, after they let him through the sealed outer area into her room, he did not get within ten feet of her bed before his wife raised both hands in warning to keep him from embracing her. 'George, don't be Sir Galahad. I know the nurse just told you not to get near me.' She made him leave the burrito dinner he brought her on a table across the room, from which she retrieved it.

Despite the required distance, it has been a companionable visit, much better than their stilted exchanges yesterday through the prison-like phones. Patrice is looking forward to her possible release tomorrow night and has offered several entertaining thoughts on what she refers to as 'life as hazmat.' But the question he just asked her was apropos of nothing, and Patrice's eyes, a penetrating blue, distinct as gemstones, flash toward him, one eyebrow encroaching on her dark forehead.

"I mean sex," he adds.

"I understood, George," she says and with that casts her eyes at the intercom rising on a separate metal stalk beside her bed. George, however, is secure. A loud bleat echoes from the speaker before the nurses' station may listen in. More to the point, his memories from the garage lie on him like a heavy stone rolled off the entrance to a tomb. He has been waiting for the right moment to discuss all this with Patrice and has spoken up suddenly, knowing the staff will shoo him out soon. The radiation-sensitive badge they pasted on his gown over his heart remains green, but the bar is shrinking.

"Did I?" he asks. He has known Patrice's story for decades. At seventeen, with a man of twenty-six, for whom she thought she had a passion. The backseat of a car. The usual squirming. Tab A. Slot B. And realizing in the aftermath that her main desire had been to get it over with and not for the smashing, handsome, worthless buddy of her older brother.

Patrice frowns, turning another page. "Not that I can recall, Georgie," she says, then adds, with typical tart understatement. "Perhaps it means something that I never asked."

He plows on, though, eager for her help.

"Well, I've been thinking about it," he says. "In the context of this case."

"What case?"

"The one with the four boys? From Glen Brae?" He forces himself to say, "The rape. I told you it was argued today." George heard a press account of the argument on the radio as he was driving here. 'Dramatic developments,' the reporter said. One judge had suggested that the entire case might be tossed out. Tape rolled of Sapperstein crowing on the courthouse steps as if Nathan Koll had not clobbered him from behind. George constantly longs for the days when public discourse was sterile and proper, and not the semaphore called spin.

"And how did that go?" Patrice asks, already forgetting what he told her on the phone this afternoon. It is one of the incurable issues between them that she takes his profession lightly. Her achievements as an architect are tangible. Buildings can stand for centuries. Beauty, above all, endures. Attorneys, by contrast, just mince around with words. But because Patrice so often sees the legal enterprise as farcical, and lawyers as a swarming scrum of uncontrolled neurotics, she enjoys George's description of the contest between Jordan Sapperstein and Nathan Koll. It's a virtual travel poster for her view of the land called Law. Even in her weariness, she laughs at length for the first time this evening.

"And where do you come out in all of this?" she asks.

"Not with Koll. Not exactly."

"So, where?"

"I don't really know. But I'm bothered. And somehow. Well—that's why I asked. About whether I told you. Because I suddenly realized that my experience was not unlike—" Now he struggles.

"Like what?" There is an undertone of alarm.

"This case. *Warnovits.*"

"Please, George. I'm sure it was nothing like it at all." She tries to sound soothing, but anger curls her voice at the edges. As she said: It means something that she never asked. She is not merely a spectator, that's what she's telling him. Sex, after all, matters. The culture screams it. Not to mention our preoccupations. Like death, it remains one of life's predetermined destinations, and thus is a land of heavy portent whenever one arrives.

In the interval, her fine features have darkened, and her gaze on him is more alert.

"Georgie, you don't seem yourself."

"Why do you say that?"

"Don't play dumb, George. It's not you to stew about cases. You're distracted. Have you found your cell phone yet?"

He's messing up. He can see that. Her needs deserve to predominate, and her clear need right now is for George to be what he always is. Poised. Stable. Loyal as a hound. It would be preposterous, after all, to ask her to feel sorry for *him* because of her brush with mortality. Worse, Patrice would take it as a breach of faith. When she leaves the hospital tomorrow, or the day after, she intends to use the term *cured*. The evil invading cells are certain to have been annihilated and thus exert no claim on their future. She wants George to lock arms with her and march forward with no looking back.

"I'm fine, mate," he answers.

A knock. His hour is up. From the door, he waves brightly.

"Home tomorrow," he says. "No more hospital."

"No more hospital," she repeats.

In the air lock between the room and the hospital corridor, George removes the paper layers that covered him and pushes them into a special bag he was given when he entered. A technician sweeps him with a bright orange hand-held Geiger counter, a device the same size as a walkie-talkie. He may go. Striding down the garishly lit hospital corridor, he passes the doorways that often frame briefly glimpsed portraits of anguish. Yet his mind remains on his wife.

When George met Patrice, he was in his third year in law school and she was a sophomore at Easton College. At a traffic light near the Easton campus, he had gazed over into an MG Roadster in the next lane, its top down in the sun, and found himself stunned by the sight of the driver. The young woman had the kind of tidy, perfect beauty that would last forever; she would still be called gorgeous at ninety. When she caught George ogling, he pretended he'd been staring at the parafoam dice that hung from the rearview mirror rather than at her.

'I've never understood what those are for,' he said through his open window. 'The dice? Is it luck?' His impression was that the toys would make it harder to see out the window.

In response, he had gotten her cool smile.

'I'll have to ask my boyfriend,' she said. 'It's his car.'

The light changed and she was gone, but the next time he saw her, at a party, she recognized him.

'I never found out about the dice,' she said. 'Somehow when you asked me, I realized that the best thing about that guy was the convertible.'

He had thought then that he was getting in on the ground floor—before hordes of fellows his age were pursuing her, perhaps even before Patrice realized how much better she could do. There is never an ounce of false modesty when George declares that he married up, took a wife who is more capable than he. But Patrice was far ahead of him—as always. She knew what he was and had plans of her own. She wanted someone solid, faithful, supportive—and impressed. She had gone to architecture school, been the standout he expected, and then heaved most of it out when their second son was born. When she resumed practice, she worked on residences—not the highest art of architecture, pop tunes when she could have been composing symphonies. But she never complained. Patrice has always known her desires in a far more determined way than most human beings.

He has reached their house in Nearing. They have lived here almost a quarter of a century, having bought the place not long after George entered private practice. It was a starter home, but over the years it became Patrice's canvas. They have undertaken four separate renovations, each one of which Patrice, unlike her husband, greeted as if it were the arrival of spring. What began as a flat-roofed Prairie-style ranch is now a two-and-a-half-story house graced with Arts and Crafts details and some touches of Wright, and is more than three times its original size.

With the taste of a burrito still somehow lodged in his salivary glands, George stops in the kitchen for a bottle of water before heading to his study to sort what the postman has delivered and to check his e-mail. George remains slightly vexed by Patrice's forbidding reaction when he compared *Warnovits* with his own encounter decades ago. His wife at moments is wont to demand perfection of him. He is, fundamentally, her beautiful George — nearly as pretty as she is, well mannered, well liked, the senior member of a family that, as one of their friends said long ago, looks as if it came off the cover of a J. Crew catalog.

This has worked out well for them, because he is equally demanding of himself, a tendency that might well have been alleviated by age, were it not for going on the bench. Judging, to George's mind, is essentially an arrogant enterprise. As a defense lawyer, he refused to condemn his clients. Everyone else in the system—the cops, the prosecutors, the juries and judges—would take care of that; they didn't need his help. But a judge's duty is to declare right and wrong, a daring undertaking, because it contains an implicit warranty that you are above the weaknesses you denounce. After remembering what happened forty years ago in a refrigerator box, he regards that as a pitiable charade.

The incident, confined to recollected fragments for decades, is now coming back to him in larger pieces. And as he settles at his desk, George abruptly recalls that it had not ended with Joan, the young woman who was to become Mario's wife, cracking wise about life.

'Sweet Christ crucified, there's a girl asleep in

the library,' the dorm proctor, Franklin Grigson, told George the following day. At 8:00 A.M., the old dorm languished in the somnolent air of a Sunday morning. Grigson and George might have been the only two young men awake after the night of partying. Grigson was heading to church. George was returning from the men's room, where he had been sick yet again. He was better now, but his head still felt like the clanger in a ringing steeple bell.

'Do us all a favor,' Grigson said. 'Find whoever she belongs to and have him get her out of here.' If the girl was discovered, the unforgiving deans would revoke parietal hours for the dorm for the balance of the semester.

George crept to the library door. It was a handsome room, wainscoted in light oak in which generations of collegians had occasionally engraved their initials. The recessed bookcases were fully encumbered with old leather-bound volumes. On the torn maroon sofa farthest from the door, a girl slept. She was a slender, auburn-haired creature, in a raveled tartan skirt. A huge hole had eaten through the calf of one leg of her sheer tights. With just a glance, George knew who she was.

Upstairs, he pounded on Hugh Brierly's door until Brierly appeared on the threshold, clad only in his pajama bottoms.

'You lie,' Brierly said. He claimed that he had escorted her to the dorm's front steps and offered to find a ride, but that the young woman was sobering up and said she would look after herself.

'You didn't take her home?' George asked. A gentleman—several of them—could have his way with a young lady in a refrigerator carton, but it was a breach of a code George had been taught was sacred not to see her back to her house.

'Don't be a pussy, Mason. I don't know where she's from. She showed up at the football game. What was I supposed to do? Escort her back to Scott?' he said, referring to the stadium.

'Well, what are you going to do now?' George asked.

'Me? You had as much to do with her as I did. You get rid of the slut,' Brierly said and shut the door. Remembering the fistful of 'rent' Brierly had collected the night before, George pounded for some time, but Hugh would not open up. To the best of George's memory, they never spoke again.

Downstairs, the young woman had awakened. She was a mess. Sitting on the threadbare Oriental carpet, she braced herself against one wall, trying to separate the patches of her long hair gummed together by the detritus of what had passed the night before. From her reddened features, he took it that she had allergies or a cold. The large gold pin that was meant to hold her wraparound kilt had been reinserted sideways, and there was a bright magenta stain from Hi-C covering the upper portion of her blouse. When she saw George in the doorway, her look was piercing.

"Whatta *you* want?"

The question, as he recalled, had struck him dumb. Because he had realized suddenly that there was in fact something he desired from her. Now, forty-some years later, sitting in the large leather desk chair that once was in his law office, George Mason is still. Along the pathways of memory, he crawls like a bomb expert creeping down a tunnel. It is a sensitive operation. A false move will destroy his chance, because he hopes for a second to inhabit the skin of that young man who was still unformed at the core. What had he wanted from her, as he stood at the threshold? Not forgiveness. It would flatter him too much to think his state of moral understanding was so far ahead of his times. In those days, it never once occurred to him that she might have been in any sense unwilling. He must have felt some lash of shame for sinning and some embarrassment at seeing her. Perhaps he was visited by an impulse to blame her, to call her names, as Brierly had. But standing twenty feet from her in the old library, preposterously, improbably, he had wanted one thing more than any other: connection. He had been with her in public, when she had been virtually insensate. But they had been joined in that fundamental way. Euclid said that a straight line is the most direct connection between two points, no matter how random or distant, and at that moment George Mason would have told you that it was a rule about sex as much as about geometry. Was it instinctive that a bounty of tenderness went with the act? Looking at her, he felt acute despair that she did not even know his name.

And so he introduced himself. He approached and, lacking any other gesture, offered his hand. She took it limply.

'I wonder if I can help you,' he said.

For all his good intentions, the question provoked a ripple of despair that briefly withered her red face before she contained herself. For reasons George understood only too well, her fingertips then pressed each of her temples.

'Get me cigarettes,' she said. She lifted the empty pack that had been squashed in her right hand and flung it at the sofa. 'I need a cigarette.'

He waited there, still feeling everything he had an instant before.

'You didn't say your name,' he told her.

She made a face but succumbed, clearly regarding this as the price she had to pay.

'Great,' she said. 'Great, George. I'm Lolly. Viccino.' She turned away and let her head fall back against the wall. 'I'm Lolly Viccino, and I'd love a cigarette.'

As he sits recalling all of this, a clear image of the four boys from Glen Brae in the front row of the courtroom this morning returns to him. Their supporters and defense lawyers have trumpeted each young man's good character over the years, and in their dark suits, their hair freshly trimmed,

Sapperstein had done his best to make them look their parts. No amount of defense burnishing can really render Jacob Warnovits appealing. He is clearly a thug with a long disciplinary record, including four earlier arrests, in high school and college. But the other three defendants, all now with their B.A.s, have each had notable achievements. One, a junior Phi Beta Kappa at an eastern college, had been planning to join the staff of a local Congresswoman until his indictment. Another was the founder of a program to teach inner-city kids to ice skate, which he still runs as a volunteer. The last, up to the time of his conviction, worked on the athletic staff at the Mid-Ten university he'd attended on a hockey scholarship.

From the bench, George had scrutinized the four. One young man was aging fast; his lank hair was thinning, and he had plumped up to the point that he no longer looked like an athlete. The judge hoped that was Warnovits, although he knew that nature seldom follows the design of justice. But the other three were handsome emblems of their potential, who watched their fates being argued with the quick, disbelieving eyes you might expect from anyone finding that one hour seven years ago still held the power to determine the rest of his life.

Seeing them in his mind's eye, George draws the contrast to the young man in the dormitory library forty years before. Why assume his character was any better than theirs? Isn't it likely that one of them—even all of them—felt some decent impulse, shame or caring for Mindy DeBoyer, in the aftermath? Not enough, of course, to set it right, to call an ambulance or her parents. But when they redressed her like a sleeping child, or bore her unconscious body down the stairs, is it possible that one or two did not respond to the warm weight of humanity?

A sound interrupts, a chirping from his computer to signal the arrival of new e-mail. He and his sons exchange messages every night about their mother, her mood and her condition. A photo of the two boys together, each buoyant and handsome, is on his desk. Patrice and he had done this part very well, although even on this subject Patrice can't resist occasional sarcasm. 'Where did I go wrong?' she asks whenever she confesses that both their sons are lawyers. Peter split the difference and practices construction law here in town. He recently became engaged. Pierce, the younger, is with a giant entertainment firm in L.A.

But as soon as the e-mail client opens, George sees that neither is his correspondent. The From and Subject lines bear the now familiar omens. The words of #1, buried after the returned-message notice, are 'Good advice,' followed by the blue letters of another link. Clicking, George finds himself at the site of a well-known life insurance company. There the page header reads: 'If you're a married man, plan accordingly. Your wife is quite likely to live longer than you.'

George closes his eyes, trying to take in the fact that #1 has invaded his home. But for the moment that seems no worse than an annoyance. His spirit has not yet fully returned from Virginia forty years before, where, like a wandering ghost, it is still dumbly seeking Lolly Viccino.

7

THE CHIEF

When George Mason drives into the Judges' Section of the parking structure on Wednesday morning, Abel Birtz is waiting by the third-floor stairway to greet him. Abel appeared in the judge's chambers late yesterday afternoon, about an hour after Marina left, heaping himself onto the green Naugahyde sofa in the reception area. 'I'm your detail, Judge,' he explained. George did his best to appear pleased.

'Sorry you have to waste your time with this, Abel.'

'Hell no, Judge. We take this serious.'

From the start, George recognized the flaw in Marina's plan to assign him a bodyguard. Court Security's resources are too strapped to waste anyone worthwhile on this kind of thumb twiddling. Abel, a former Kindle copper, is garrulous and inoffensive, but he has gone to pasture. His khaki sport coat, emblazoned at the pocket with the court's seal, would need another yard of fabric to close across his massive belly. Greeting the judge yesterday, he required several attempts to hike himself forward on the sofa cushion before arriving on his feet, his large, square face considerably reddened. And he clearly has an arthritic hip. He walks with a swinging gait as they cross the covered gangway between the parking garage and the courthouse. God help them both, George thinks, if #1 strikes and they need to run for their lives.

And there is another problem with Abel's presence, which does not strike George until he takes in the vexed look with which Dineesha greets him as they push through the door to chambers. Though it is no fault of either, Dineesha and Abel have an uncomfortable history.

George and Patrice first met Dineesha more

than two decades ago at PTA meetings, which Dineesha attended as the mother of Jeb, a scholarship student at the Morris School. Jeb, who now practices rehabilitative medicine in Denver, was in the same fourth-grade class as Peter, the Masons' elder son. But it was Dineesha's oldest boy, Zeke, who served to fortify her relationship with George. Knowing what he did for a living, Dineesha sought George out when Zeke was arrested. It was not Zeke's first bust, but these charges, for having supposedly joined other gangbangers in burning down the apartment of a young man attempting to quit, carried a mandatory prison term. It was a bad beef on a bad kid, mud the cops were willing to throw at the wall because it was time something stuck. Maybe Zeke had been there, but if so, George became convinced he was merely a spectator.

George took the case without fee and won, but Dineesha insisted on doing overflow typing in his office as a form of payment. She was soon a permanent addition to George's practice—and so was Zeke. As a first-year in Charlottesville, George had fought fiercely with classmates about the Civil Rights Act, which he was sure would leave the path to progress for Negroes unimpeded. Work hard. Play by the rules. Get an education. He had no understanding of the perils for young black men, even those like Zeke, who could not have been raised by more loving or ambitious parents. Who knew where Zeke's problems started? Probably by being less academically gifted than his two younger sibs. It is an inevitable rule of family life, as George sees it, that children occupy the space provided, and in Dineesha's house the available space turned out to be a cell in Rudyard penitentiary, where Zeke has been twice. Back on the street at the moment, he still shows up at his parents' home often for a meal and money. George has given up his lectures to his assistant on tough love. But the sight of Abel ten feet from Dineesha's desk can only refresh her heartbreak. It was Abel Birtz, then a property crimes detective, who pinched Zeke on the burglary bit that first led him to do time.

George is sure that all of this is wrapped up in the baleful look they received coming through the door, but Dineesha has another reason to be bothered by the leisurely way her boss is chatting with Abel. She taps her watch.

"The Chief Judge?" she reminds him. "The High Court?"

"Yikes!" George turns and runs.

To mute the protests of the appellate judges about moving to the bleak wilderness beyond U.S. 843, the County Board constructed a small athletic facility, including a racquetball court, which was added only because it was a perfect use of a large air shaft at the center of the double floor. It has been dubbed 'the High Court' by wags. Handball can also be played here, and the Chief Judge, Rusty Sabich, still prefers the older game, smashing a small rubber ball around with gloved palms. He and George have matches twice a week.

"Georgie boy!" The Chief is slipping into his athletic shorts in the tiny locker room when Judge Mason dashes in, spouting apologies. The two have enjoyed a solid friendship throughout their professional lives. Sabich was the Deputy Prosecuting Attorney in the courtroom to which George was initially assigned as a State Defender, and for the first three months, Rusty often whispered helpful suggestions as they stood before Judge White. 'Move for a speedy trial.' 'Remind him the parents will put their house up to secure bail.' In time, they also had their share of battles, but going toe to toe in court often seals a friendship once the sting of losing has passed. Rusty, who wields considerable political swack, was the prime mover when George was offered the chance to run for this job more than ten years ago.

"I need to talk to you," the Chief says.

"We're on top of term deadline," George answers. One of Rusty's many reforms in the court is a rule requiring all argued cases to be decided by the conclusion of the court's annual term, two weeks from now. It ended the former practice under which decisions that might disappoint political heavyweights remained in limbo for years. The requirement also forces the judges to keep up with their opinions through the year to avoid an impossible backlog now. But that is not what's on Rusty's mind.

"Couple other items," he answers.

They have moved into the lavatory, where George is soaking his hands in warm water to diminish the chance of bruising. The Chief stands by, heavy goggles already in place, squeezing the handball to soften it.

"Number One," he says and stops on the words. A smile flashes by like a fish through the water. "Not to joke, Georgie. It's a serious matter."

"Rusty," George says—he addresses the Chief by first name only in private—"how the hell did you hear about that?"

"Marina told me last night. Chilling," the Chief adds, "especially if she's right about Corazón. The only way he could engineer something like this, in my opinion, is if the Almighty Latin Nation turned a guard. And Corrections did everything but a genealogy chart for every staff member in the super-max. These gangs can probably reach as far as the mob in the old days."

"Rusty, I specifically asked Marina not to talk about this with anybody but me, and especially not about Corazón. I don't need my staff any jumpier, and frankly, I don't give the idea much credence." Even less since last night's e-mail. No matter what the influence of ALN or Corazón's set, Latinos Reyes, how would any of them know about Patrice's illness? Nonetheless, the reality that Marina is beyond his control puts to rest any thought of telling her about the message. There would be investigators crawling all over the house and twenty-four-hour bodyguards, not a scene he would even consider bringing his ailing wife home to.

"Easy, Georgie. I'm her boss. And besides, she thinks we may find a little silver lining here."

"Which is?"

"Well, it gives her a case in point to press the County Board for an emergency-funding authorization for increased courthouse security."

"And I'm the poster child?" George does not try to hide his irritation. He's been keeping this a secret in his household, and now Marina, who clearly has her own agenda, wants to make him the lead item in the Metro Section.

"Hardly," Rusty says. "Hardly. We'll explain to the Board without names. But after the murder in Cincinnati, this gives us a wedge to get some dollars back. Let them hire a few less flunkies to patrol the Public Forest."

Marina likes to joke that last year the Board made her reduce her two-man security patrols in the garage to one officer and a German shepherd, and this year they want to replace the shepherd with a Chihuahua. And with #1's threats as evidence, Rusty may be able to convince the County Board to restore funds, since they often defer to his reputation.

It's sometimes hard to explain to younger people how Rusty Sabich came to be the public embodiment of probity, inasmuch as nearly twenty years ago, while he was the Chief Deputy Prosecutor, Rusty was indicted and tried for the murder of a female colleague. From the start, George had stood by him, and was not surprised when the case presented against Rusty turned out to be an outright embarrassment, a mishmash of bad lab work, missing evidence, and unreliable witnesses. The only lingering debate today is whether the then newly elected P.A., who saw Rusty as a potential rival, framed him or, as George believes, was simply far too eager to reach the wrong conclusions.

Either way, as the acknowledged victim of a horrible injustice, Sabich had singular qualifications to be a judge. He was elected to this court in 1988, then propelled to Chief by the same courthouse scandal that first swept George onto the bench. Rusty is regarded as a sure thing for the state Supreme Court, whenever Ned Halsey surrenders what is colloquially referred to as "the white man's seat," in distinction to the two other spots on the Court reserved for Kindle County, which are filled in accordance with recent political understandings by a racial minority and a woman.

But there remains an air of aloofness to Rusty, which at times borders on pretension. Once accused of murder, he is forever straightening his spine. His life is as neatly divided by the experience as if someone had painted a stripe through it. George understands but occasionally dislikes who Rusty has become in the aftermath, often depressed and some-times officious, as he was just now about Marina, and almost always on guard. That said, he has been an extraordinary Chief Judge. He became an able manager running the P.A.'s office, and he has used his public stature to wrest control of this court from the party chieftains, transforming it into a respected judicial body.

Together now they hunch to enter the half-height door to the High Court. They are well

matched physically, both tallish, fit, and gray. Rusty
has bulked up a little more with age, and George
may be a bit faster now, but that does not make up
for what Rusty learned by playing this game since
he was a boy, an ingrained intuition about how
every ball will carom. He wins consistently and
by long agreement spots George points, two in
the games to twenty-one, one if the match goes
to the eleven-point tiebreaker. Still agitated about
Marina, George plays with fury and wins the first
game straight up, 21 to 17.

"You're not going to have anything left for game
two," Rusty says when they take a breather at the
watercooler.

"Trash-talk somebody else, you old fart. I think
you've finally lost a step."

"Another one," Sabich says.

George rests his hands on his knees. Rusty is
right that he pushed himself hard.

"So here's my next item, George. What's the
deal with your retention petition?"

"I have two weeks."

"Formally," Rusty answers. "But look, George.
There are a hundred and fifty judges in the Superior

Court who'd like to move up. You've been there. Everybody gets sick of the grind. Trials. Motions. Lawyers with all their cockamamie. I've gotten six calls this week. Not to mention Nathan."

"Koll?" Nathan's seat is being eliminated for budgetary reasons, which is what led Jerry Ryan, the judge elected to the position, to resign in pique. Nathan will not be eligible simply to seek retention.

"Just because his appointment lasts two more years doesn't mean he can't run for a full-term seat if a vacancy develops now. I bet he sends his clerks downstairs twice a day to see if you've filed. George, you can't do *that* to us. We're your friends." Rusty is smiling. It was he who encouraged the Supreme Court to give the interim appointment to Nathan, thinking that the addition of a famous legal scholar would be another enhancement to the stature of the court. These days, he says he'd like to donate Nathan's body to science—while he's still living. "Seriously, George. We need you around here. Don't let this hairball's threats give you second thoughts about staying on."

There is an unspoken issue. Rusty has controlled

membership on the court for more than a decade and does not want anybody making an end run around him. If George were uninterested in retention, he owed the Chief word of that long ago.

"It's not that, Rusty. I've just been waiting for all the dust to settle with Patrice."

"Sure. But raising false hopes, you'll end up making enemies you don't need. Get the papers filed. And speaking of Nathan, what's he up to on *Warnovits*? I read a bizarre item in the *Tribune* about your oral argument yesterday."

Like everybody else, Rusty finds the story of Koll's sneak attack on Sapperstein hilarious.

"So he's going to dissent on those grounds?" Rusty asks.

"Or concur separately."

The idea that George might vote to reverse catches the Chief short.

"I think the limitations issue is tough, Rusty."

"Really?" Sabich's eyes are open wide as he calculates. Among Rusty's concerns as Chief is maintaining public respect for the court's decisions. But there is a line here. The judges often ask one another about abstract legal issues, but it is out of bounds for a judge not sitting on a case to suggest an outcome.

With no more said, Rusty waves George back onto the court. Halfway through the second game, with the score 10–10, George realizes that he does not have the juice to go on to a tiebreaker. His only hope for the match is to take this game. Before each point he stops to fill his lungs, exhorting himself to press all-out. Ahead 20 to 19, with the serve, George ends a long rally with a desperate lunge for a great passing shot Rusty has hit. The ball flips off George's fingertips, arching up like a diver and plunging in slow motion to strike the very base of the front wall. George has won.

"Oh, for God's sake," Rusty says. George has not beaten him two games to naught all year.

George collects the ball and finds Rusty with his hand on the door.

"So let me understand this. Koll votes to reverse because the videotape was inadmissible, you vote to reverse because of limitations, and Summer dissents on both grounds. Is that how this is breaking down?"

George sags a little, realizing that his triumph was due in part to the Chief's distraction with *Warnovits*.

"That's one scenario. I took the opinion, and I have no clue yet what I'm going to do, Russ."

"Well, that's a relief. Look, George, don't let Nathan mousetrap you on this thing."

"'Mousetrap'?"

"Play it out. Reverse on limitations grounds and what happens to the case?"

"*Finito.*"

"Right. But Nathan's grounds?"

George shrugs. He's never gotten that far in his own mind.

"Think about it," the Chief says. "If you guys hold only that the tape was inadmissible, the prosecutors will be able to go back to square one. You'll already have decided that there's no limitations bar, and so under the statute, the P.A.'s office gets one year from the reversal to reindict the case with any violations that spring from the same criminal transaction. Right so far?"

"I'm following."

"Which means the prosecutors will charge all

four of these men for eavesdropping. Correct? Then the P.A.s will wait to see which defendant bangs down their door first to make a deal to testify about the rape. The worst of those boys will be charged with both crimes. And everybody ends up with convictions. Justice delayed," Rusty says, "but not denied.

"But go where you're headed? Three separate opinions? We should just dial 911 right now. The case gets reversed without any guidance to the trial court on whether it can go forward. Either we rehear it en banc or, better bet, the Supreme Court steps in. And then you're running for retention after deciding in a marquee case that you'll free four rich white rapists on a technicality, in an opinion which no other judge would join and which, odds on, gets overturned. I mean, Jesus, George. Talk about looking for trouble." Rusty touches the sodden shoulder of George's T-shirt. "Ask yourself if Nathan didn't play all that out in his head before he got on the bench yesterday. He's going to leave you hanging from the yardarm and run for your seat when it goes south on you."

Lecture complete, Rusty exits, leaving George

within the high, white space, greatly unsettled. He is unconvinced about Koll. The complex calculations Rusty described are well within Nathan's capabilities. But the compromises are not. Koll's story to himself is that the law is a matter of rigorous reason untouched by personal motives. Once falsely accused of murder, Rusty is understandably prone to see devious and complex schemes to undermine him and his friends.

Yet about the practical consequences if George votes to reverse on limitations grounds, the Chief is clearly correct. Feminists and minorities, liberals and conservatives—a judge who manages to antagonize all those groups at once is looking for trouble on Election Day. George is as practical as the next person, but he'd as soon not run as trim his conscience to fit the ballot box.

That, he realizes, is what's bothering him most. The conversation went well past the point of propriety. George sees this with Rusty now and then. He is so accustomed to his role as the very figure of integrity that he assumes his every word and act, no matter what their character, is clothed in rectitude.

To his credit, Rusty himself has had second

thoughts by the time George reaches the locker room. Sabich is sitting on the narrow wooden bench between the banks of lockers, a towel indenting his softening middle, his chin drooped onto the gray hairs of his chest.

"George, at some point there I should have put a sock in my mouth. Let's strike all that from the record. I'm really sorry."

"No problem."

"I'm concerned for your sake. You know that."

"I do." George believes that, although Rusty's deepest concerns will always be for the court, which is his monument. "Rusty, I've disregarded your views for thirty years. It's force of habit by now."

They both smile.

"It's a hard case, Rusty. I'm having a lot of trouble with it."

"Going back and forth?"

He isn't going anywhere. After the memories of yesterday, he is unwilling even to approach a decision until he is more settled with himself.

"How is Patrice?" the Chief Judge then asks. George decides that this is not a non sequitur. It's how Rusty is explaining things to himself. Patrice is sick. George's trolley is a little off the tracks. And he might be right. George gives a brief medical update. The doctor said this morning that he expects to discharge Patrice tonight.

"Great, great," says Rusty, then the two men, now seated next to each other on the locker-room bench, subside to a silence in which *Warnovits* somehow remains the subject.

"Rusty," George eventually asks, "is a judge disqualified if something in a case reminds him of himself?"

Only after speaking does George realize how loaded the question is. Rusty at moments must see his own reflection in the face of every soul accused.

"They're supposed to remind us of ourselves, aren't they, George? Isn't that a quality of mercy?" The Chief stands then, offering his hand as a token of reassurance. "You kicked my butt," he says.

"I sure did."

"And whatever you do on that case will be the right thing."

George shakes his head, unconvinced. "It's just—" he says.

"What?"

"Don't you wonder sometimes?"

"What?"

When George finishes, he can see from the abrupt darkening of Rusty's eyes that he has said the most upsetting thing yet.

"Who are we?" George has asked his friend. "Who are we to judge?"

8
A DRAFT

"Koll's clerk told me we got the *Warnovits* opinion," says Cassandra Oakey, sweeping into the judge's large inner chambers moments after George arrives Thursday morning. "So what's the deal?"

"The deal?"

"Well, what are we doing with the case? I checked with John. You haven't assigned either one of us to start a draft. Term ends in two weeks."

Cassie is the judge's rotating law clerk. The other position, held by John Banion, is permanent, but Cassie's job is filled annually by a graduating law student. Two weeks hence, a law reviewer from Northwestern will start, and after training him for ten days, Cassie will begin work for a foundation that represents indigent immigrants. She is destined for great things in the law, but the judge cannot say he'll be sad to see her go. He has known Cassie, the daughter of Harrison Oakey, one of George's former law partners and dearest friends, since she was kicking in her mother's belly, and for her sake he set aside his standard reservations about hiring someone so close. Many of his colleagues do it, and Cassie was amply qualified. She was a standout law student who actually flattered George by accepting his clerkship over another she'd been offered in federal court. Her research and writing have proven to be flawless.

But Cassie is one of those roundly gifted people—brilliant, a former tennis star, a tall, striking ash blond—whom the world has rebuffed so infrequently that she has learned virtually nothing about boundaries. She speaks out of turn and without thinking—often with a regal air, as if it were she who's on the bench. She charges into the judge's private chambers without knocking, as she has just done, and despite frequent corrections, still calls him George in front of others, a liberty even Dineesha no longer permits herself. Now and then, George feels like a lion tamer who needs to grab a chair to keep Cassie at bay.

"I mean," she says, stepping closer to the judge's large desk, "we're affirming, right?" To Cassie, a young woman of her times, the case is open and shut. When he hesitates, his clerk's mouth droops open a bit. "Shut *up*! You're not going with Koll, are you? About the tape being inadmissible? That's totally whacked, right? We can't consider new issues now."

"I'm still turning some things over in my mind, Cassie."

"Really? Like what?"

Lord God of mercy, he thinks. Less than four weeks.

"The statute of limitations bothers me. I've read it over thirty times. It says that if the defendants engage in acts of concealment, the statute's time limit is suspended, quote, 'during such period that

those acts prevent the crime from being known.'
Unquote. But this young woman told her best friend
she might have been raped."

"I thought the trial judge said she was too young
to know enough to go to the cops."

"That's what he said. But Sapperstein has a
point. The legislature created another limitations
exception to deal with crimes against minors, but it
doesn't last forever. Once you're eighteen, and pre-
sumably old enough to understand the ways of the
world, you have a year to go to the authorities.
Mindy DeBoyer didn't do that. Is it right to allow
the trial judge to rely on her age to extend the
statute longer than the exception for crimes against
minors allows?"

"Oh," Cassie says. Apparently she has no quick
rejoinder. "Well, should I do two drafts? One affirming, one reversing on limitations grounds?"

"John wrote the bench memo, Cassie." Ordinarily the clerk who prepares the case for oral argument
drafts the judge's opinion. For *Warnovits*, besides
summarizing the tape, Banion had done the extra
research George requested about the statute of
limitations.

"John said he didn't care. I've got a little more time right now."

Cassie is not democratic—she always wants the most interesting work. Banion must be nettled, but he is uncomplaining by character. Nonetheless, the judge has struggled for months to make sure Cassie doesn't run over John and says that he will discuss all this with Banion first.

Cassie nods but stands her ground, her full face still clouded beneath the bangs of her blunt Dutch boy hairdo.

"Can I say something?" she asks and predictably does not await an answer. "I really don't understand how you can just let these guys go. They've had every break in life. They don't deserve one more."

"It's not a matter of what they deserve. People get away with things all the time, Cassie. The law can't dispense justice to every guilty person."

"But the law's not supposed to favor that, is it?"

"Then why do we require proof beyond a reasonable doubt? Why is there a statute of limitations?"

"If you ask me, I don't think there should be. Not when there's a videotape."

"First of all, I'm not the legislature."

She repeats the last four words with him. Apparently he has worn out the grooves on that one in the last year. He knows from Cassie's prior comments that she finds it a bit cowardly to hide behind the state lawmakers. And she's right that at times such claims sound like a judicial version of 'I'm only following orders.' But to George, nothing about judging is more important than refusing to be a law unto yourself.

"And second," he continues, "the law for centuries has made a judgment that, after a certain amount of time, every bad guy, except for a murderer, is entitled to go on with his life and not dwell in the shadow of past mistakes. Imagine that the videotape had turned up forty years later instead of four," he says. The example comes to him instantly, the reason so obvious that he's surprised his voice emerged without a telltale quiver. "The way the trial judge read the concealment provision, the defendants could still be prosecuted decades from now. Would you like to see them in court then?"

"You mean when they're all old men?"

"Let's be delicate"—George smiles—"and say middle-aged. But if you don't want the concealment provision to allow prosecution forty years later, why permit it today? How do the words that the legislature wrote change meaning simply through the passage of time?"

She waves her blond head back and forth, unwilling to say one way or the other.

"Come on, Judge," he says. "Decide."

Cassie presumes on their lifetime acquaintance and sticks out her tongue by way of reply, briskly departing to the adjoining office. The judge turns to the window. The trees in the parkway below have passed from the winsome colors of spring to the more declarative shades of summer.

He knows Cassie is correct about one thing. They need a decision. In the end, this job really has only one essential requirement: Make up your mind. And don't look back. Decisiveness in many ways is more important than being right. A couple of times each year, George is reversed by the state Supreme Court, whose downstate contingent often delights in putting the big-city judges in their places. It stings, but all you can say is, 'That's what they think.' Power alone makes the Supremes correct. The law at those moments feels as arbitrary as a dream. But there's no process at all without a decision.

Yet when he tries to force himself back to the *Warnovits* case, he cannot escape his own stake in it. His reflections return him instantly to Virginia, and the dormitory library where he encountered Lolly Viccino the morning after. Responding to her request for cigarettes, George had come back from the canteen with a package of Winstons, as well as a fried-egg sandwich and a nickel Coke. She ate wolfishly, then dabbed a napkin daintily at the corners of her mouth before using it to dry her running nose.

'At least there's one gentleman around here,' she said. 'The girls said all the boys down here were real gentlemen, and I decided I'd go see for myself.' She worried her head at that thought. That was as close as they were ever to come to speaking about the night before. He did not know then, or now, what portion of the events she remembered or how clearly. Lolly lit a cigarette and quickly veiled herself in smoke.

'I was wondering,' he said.

'Yeah?'

'If I could give you a hand getting home?'

Her face flashed to him. Clearly he had offended her, making it sound as if she were unwelcome. He expected a rebuke, but in a second her small brown eyes, initially hard as glass, were swimming. She crushed her hand to her nose and with a single gasp began to cry. That explained her appearance, George realized, the rheumy eyes, the drooling nose. Her look was that of someone who'd been crying for days.

She pulled the sleeve of her blouse over the heel of her palm and wiped her face with it.

'Just go away,' she told him. She swore, repeating the direction.

When he checked back in an hour, she had not moved. She was leaning against the oak paneling, smoking. Nearly half the pack was gone. She gave George a lethal look, then, recognizing him, grimaced as if to withdraw it. Apparently other young men had awoken and gawked from the library's threshold.

He sat on the floor beside her.

'My life stinks,' she said. 'You can't believe how much my life stinks.'

'Because?'

'I flunked out of Columa this week,' she said, referring to the women's college down the road. 'I mean, I was "asked to leave." You know how they put things.'

'Sure.'

'It's not as if I studied. I knew it was going to happen. But—' She began to cry again. The way she went from hard to soft in a bare instant baffled him. But this time she managed to eke out the story. It was fairly simple: she had nowhere to go. Her father deserted the family a decade before. Last year, her mother met a man, and as soon as Lolly left for college, they married. Now the mother did not want her daughter to return for more than a day or two. She wasn't going to bear the brunt of Lolly's failures by putting her new marriage under any unneeded strain. Lolly would have to make do on her own.

At the time, George sensed there was much here he was too young to fully comprehend. It was unimaginable that his parents would ever spurn him this way. He knew the kinds of adjectives his mother would reflexively apply to families like Lolly's. But what he could not fully absorb then was what she had told him about herself. He was yet to see hundreds, even thousands, of young people turn rejection into self-loathing, a force of indiscriminate destructiveness. Nothing that had happened to Lolly Viccino the day and night before was a mystery to George Mason now.

Then he understood only that she was unhappier than he was. He was always frightened by friends and classmates sunk in misery. It was an omen. A few wrong turns in his own mental fun house, and he could be similarly overwhelmed. His disagreements with his strict father, his mother's disappointments—if he surrendered to them fully, he could be like this girl, a village in flames. And so he sat beside Lolly Viccino in silence for several minutes, lecturing himself with various Christian sayings his father would have employed but still inexpressibly relieved not to be her.

9

SOMEBODY'S CHILD

At the end of term, the work flow is heavy. Drafts of opinions arrive from almost every other chamber in the court, and George has to make prudential decisions about which are worth a special word from him by way of concurrence or dissent, bearing in mind the limits on what either he or the clerks can get done in the time remaining.

By Thursday afternoon he has not left his chair, even for lunch. He has interrupted himself only for calls to Patrice. He brought her home last night, but she remains under restrictions for three more days.

She may not go out, since she must yet remain several feet from other people. In the same vein, the doctors insist that for the next three nights George and she should not share the same bed. They both enjoyed their jokes about radioactive love, but despite a longing glance, Patrice ultimately pointed him to the study, where he slept on the pullout sofa. The good news is that she is starting to feel less lethargic since being allowed to restart the synthetic thyroxine.

About to reach for the phone again, George is surprised by a squall of angry voices resounding from the corridor. John and Cassie look into his chambers from their small adjoining office, then run for the hall. George follows. Dineesha is there too. Abel is having words with a man. He looks close to thirty and is, as they say, 'g'd up' in full banger regalia: shiny white starter jacket, sagging trousers, rows, and a derringer-size pistol in gold around his neck. Urgent voices screech from the radio on Abel's belt as the young man swats at him every time Abel reaches for him. The banger knows the part about a good offense being the best defense.

"Get yo' fuckin' dogs back, Chuck, otherwise they gone be some drama."

The elevator dings, and two more khaki officers come tearing down the marble corridor. In an instant, another car delivers three additional members of Court Security. All have their radios on at full volume, and the young man is quickly surrounded and cuffed.

"I asked him ten times what he was doing here," Abel tells Murph Jones, a tall black man who is Marina's second in command.

"I was lookin' for the baf'room," the guy in cuffs responds.

"Plenty of men's rooms downstairs," Abel says. Access to the appellate court's separate elevators is restricted, with khaki guards requiring ID in the lobby from anyone trying to go up. But the stairwells on either side of the building are open because of the fire code. Strangers, including many who look like this young man, are walking around up here all the time, even ambling down the judges' private corridor.

"It's a crowd down there," he says. During the

SCOTT TUROW

10:00 A.M. court calls, the lower floors housing the
criminal courtrooms teem like a rush-hour bus
station. "I gotta go."

"And what brought you downstairs?" Murph
asks.

"You know, man. Got a turnout. On a case." He
means he has a required court appearance on a
pending charge. The point is to be sure he hasn't
skipped bail.

"What kind of beef?" Murph asks.

"Some rudipoop 323. I ain' gone catch no bit
for it." Mob Action is the violation he's referring to.
Living while being a banger. Men on a corner
representing, or cruising a drive-by. The cops grab
them to prevent trouble, but the charges never stick,
just as this young fellow has said.

"Take him down," Murph says.

"Oh, man," the banger answers. "Ain't that
America or what? Gone get rolled up for goin'
tinkle."

They'll hold him most of the day, but if everything checks out, they'll have to let him go, probably
by nightfall. Four of the khaki officers take hold of
the young man but do not get far down the corridor.

134

They are halted by the arrival of Marina, who holds up a hand to signal that she is taking over, even as she's dashing forward with a surprisingly athletic bound. When she gets to George, she asks if he is okay.

"Nothing happened to me," George says. "Abel's the hero." He was sprier than George had expected.

"Punk like that," Abel says but doesn't finish the sentence.

"I don't like this, Judge," Marina says after she's been briefed. "I'm thinking Corazón." She's lowered her voice so that the banger, a distance down the hall, cannot hear her, but the name George has asked her not to mention is still audible to his staff arrayed along the wall. Listening, Dineesha, John, Cassie, Marcus, the courtroom bailiff all look up at the same time.

"Marina, that kid is black. He's not courted in to ALN. Did you see a star, Abel?" All jumped-in members of the Almighty Latin Nation sport a five-pointed star tattooed between the wrist and thumb.

"Saint," Abel says. "He got the Chinese junk on his hand." The Black Saints Disciples' tats in the last few years have gone to Chinese characters, because the cops have a hard time telling apart the marks of one set or another.

"The Latin and black gangs—they're oil and water," George says.

"Come on, Judge. You know the deals the gangs make in the joint as well as I do. They trade cappings. Gives the obvious suspects an alibi when the target goes down. Corazón realizes we'd be looking for a Latino."

Marina's right about the gang sociology, but that doesn't make this man Corazón's emissary. For one thing, he was unarmed. Yet the incident is discomfiting, because the judge doubts the tale about the bathroom. The guy was up here scoping things out—but theft, rather than violence, might have been his motive, or just a renegade desire to go where he was unwelcome. Nonetheless, it's the first vague indication that #1's presence might reach beyond the electronic fantasyland of the Internet.

The officers have resumed leading the gangbanger away when a voice resounds from the other end of the judges' private corridor.

"Whoa," someone says. "Whoa. What you-all doin' with my road dog there?"

A large figure advances confidently down the hallway. His attire is a more polished version of what the young man being held has on, the same baggies and jacket but less gold, and he sports a Lycra wig cap, similar to those worn by long-haired football players under their helmets. Dineesha makes a sound first, but George recognizes the man at almost the same moment. So does Abel, who can't suppress a hawking groan from the back of his throat. It's Zeke, Dineesha's oldest son.

Zeke is still Zeke, big and affable, a gifted talker. "Hey there, Mr. Mason. Momma," he says and manages to peck his mother's cheek in the same motion in which he reaches for George's hand.

"Judge," murmurs Dineesha, correcting him, and without another word departs. Zeke watches her go with a timeworn smile. Nearly six three, he must be going close to three hundred these days. He has grown out a kinky stubble on his face as some kind of fashion statement.

The contours of Zeke's story match fairly well with his friend's. He accompanied this buddy, Khaleel, to the courthouse for his appearance, just to be sociable. When Khaleel couldn't find a free spot in the crowded men's room downstairs, Zeke directed him up here. He knows the layout of the floor, of course, from his visits to his mother.

"A little strange," says Marina, "that you didn't stop by to say hi to your mom."

Zeke just laughs at that. "Don't want to bother her when she's workin'," he says.

George's pinball tilts on with that one. Zeke comes around often—too often as far as his mother's concerned—walking through chambers and greeting everyone as if they'd been waiting for him to stop in to sign autographs. It's obvious that Zeke sent Khaleel up here for another reason. Maybe Khaleel was supposed to see if Dineesha was working so Zeke could corner her for money, or perhaps it was to be sure she wasn't there so Zeke could prevail on George for a favor. Or perhaps, as Marina is certain to believe, he was up to something more sinister. It doesn't matter. The two men have their stories down, leaving no real basis to hold either. Not that that would stop Marina's people or anybody else in law enforcement from locking them up for a while anyway, in other circumstances. But now the two are no longer simply badass bangers. Zeke is somebody's child. The cuffs are removed, and the two friends amble off down the corridor, clearly pleased with themselves.

"You know what I'm thinking," Marina says to George. He lets her lay it out once he's motioned his staff to go back inside. Corazón found Zeke through the gang networks she described before, and Zeke was here to direct a surveillance on George, planning for some event. "Let's check up on both of them," Marina says quietly to Murph before she departs.

Back in George's chambers, there are no voices amid a funereal mood of fear and sympathy for Dineesha. She has deserted her desk. George thinks she may have slipped out or is in with Cassie and Banion, but he finds her inside the door to his private chambers, sitting alone in a straight-backed chair. She has a hankie in her hand, but the crying for now appears to be over.

"Judge, I am so sorry."

"For what? He didn't do anything."

She answers with a look.

George still regards Marina's theory of gang alliances as fanciful. But there is no denying that

Zeke deserves to be a suspect in his own right. There's no limit to what Zeke knows about George, both through their contacts over the years as lawyer and client, and far more, from what he hears through his mother. Who knows which of the eternal resentments always seething in Zeke might have spurred an effort to intimidate George? Some theory that George has misused Dineesha for the last two decades. Or yet another way for Zeke to revenge himself on her. Or some long-simmering bitch about the way George represented him. The judge knows that among the many educational projects that took Zeke nowhere in life was training as a computer programmer after his first stretch at Rudyard. If Zeke is #1, then he probably sent Khaleel up here to lift something, or to check out a piece of information Zeke would stick in his next unpleasant message.

But even were that the case, there is comfort to be taken, because George would be in absolutely no danger. Zeke is a con, a crook, an inveterate swindler whose dominating passion is to prove he can put it over on everybody else. His performance in the hallway, talking Khaleel out of handcuffs, is vintage Zeke, a moment he'll be celebrating and recounting for days. But there's nothing on his long sheet involving any real violence, notwithstanding the behavior of many of those with whom he's surrounded himself. If it's Zeke, then all of these threats are aimed at a payoff of some kind, an inventive scam he's preparing to run. A ransom for stopping. A reward for information, or for investigative services. Some setup.

There is no telling Dineesha that Zeke had innocent motives today or that he's not a suspect for #1. She has already assumed the worst and sits rigidly in the chair, plainly suffering.

"My own child," she finally says to George before she gets up to return to her desk.

LOST AND FOUND

his house and remains a few lengths behind until he reaches Independence Boulevard, the brewery on which becomes the river flow into the ... in every morning. Lots of people drive past the West Bank into the Center City at 8:30 a.m., he tells himself, and maybe... he does the surface street to avoid the ... of the highway. But then he gets a

10

LOST AND FOUND

Not long after he leaves home Friday morning, Judge Mason concludes he's being followed. A car, a late-model maroon DeVille, appears in his rearview mirror when he's no more than a block away from his house and remains a few lengths behind until he reaches Independence Boulevard, the byway on which he crosses the river Kindle into the city every morning. Lots of people drive from the West Bank into the Center City at 8:30 A.M., he tells himself, and many, as he does, use surface streets to avoid the tie-ups on the highway. But when he gets a better look, the car concerns him. It's 'pimped out,' as the cops would put it, with the suspension lowered and a fringe swinging in the rear window. A vapor trail has been detailed on each fender, and the auto is topped with an old-fashioned leather carriage roof in cream. Standard gangster ride. He's a bit relieved when the Cadillac finally disappears. No more than five minutes later, it's there again, jumping in and out of lanes a quarter of a block behind him.

He turns down the radio so he can concentrate and moves into the right lane, traveling about twenty miles per hour. The Caddy slows up as well. After another couple of minutes, he hooks a right onto Washburn and shoots several blocks down the narrow streets in the neighborhood of three-flats. The DeVille is gone. But when he circles back onto Independence, the Cadillac zooms out of an alley and closes again to four or five car lengths.

A half mile farther on, the judge pulls his Lexus to the curb, and the Caddy comes to rest in a red zone a hundred feet behind. When George steals back into the traffic, the car does too. Finally, no more than three blocks from the courthouse, he stops short at a light, leaving the Cadillac without a choice about pulling up beside him.

The driver is a slick-looking young man, white or Hispanic, with black spiked hair. He's wearing a leather vest. A portly black man in a coat and tie occupies the passenger's seat. The young man flashes George a tidy smile and winks.

His heart gives a frightened spurt before he understands, then he flashes a quick okay sign, thumb and forefinger. But he's burning. Unwilling to wait until he gets to chambers, he curbs the car again so he can dial the cell phone he's borrowed from his wife.

"We had an agreement," he tells Marina as soon as she answers her private line.

"What?"

"You made a deal with me, Marina. I was only going to be covered in the courthouse. I've just had two county cops riding my tail from home in a Caddy they forfeited from some dope king."

Marina is quiet. "You weren't supposed to pick them up."

"In that car? It's for undercover buys in the North End. In my neighborhood, they might as well have announced themselves with heralds. Really, Marina. What the hell are you up to?"

"Judge, I'm just trying to do the right thing. After those two characters showed up out in the corridor yesterday, I thought things were getting a little close for comfort. I called a pal of mine, Don Stanley, and asked them to keep an eye on you, back and forth. No details, Judge. I said we had an incident that made me a little hinky." She's clearly talked to Rusty, who let her know that George does not take kindly to her talking out of school. That would be particularly true about sharing information with the Kindle County cops. Rumors and gossip are traded faster than in a junior high at the police head-quarters, McGrath Hall. If word gets out about #1, it would find its way quickly to a reporter.

"Marina, I'm the one who's on the line here. And so I make the choices. When they find my body, I give you permission to hold a press conference right over the remains and say, 'I told him so.'"

"Come on, Judge."

"Marina, on my block there are nine families who've lived there for twenty years. We raised our kids together. We vacation together. We pick up one another's newspapers and mail. None of us minds his own business. And there's no way these lugs in a dope-mobile following me from home each morning—or back—aren't going to be noticed. Tomorrow or the day after, one of my neighbors is certain to say something to Patrice."

He struggles to rein in his temper, reminding himself that Marina's intuition that #1 may have a bead on his house is more accurate than she knows. But the last thing he'll do at this stage is mention that e-mail. He already has virtually no handle on her. And overnight he's grown more settled that Zeke is the culprit. Nevertheless, he tries a more patient approach.

"Marina, I realize you don't know Patrice all that well. So let me explain. She's one of those people who go rock climbing and then come home and throw the dead bolt and set the burglar alarm. She designs houses. She thinks everybody is entitled to a safe private space. This would upset her at the best of times. And it's not the best of times."

"I understand, Your Honor. Only—" She stops.

"What?"

"You know, not to get in the middle, Judge, but maybe we can work out security arrangements that wouldn't alarm Mrs. Mason. Might even make her more comfortable. Because I really think it'd be better for everyone, including the two of you, if she knew what was going on."

His efforts at self-control prove futile.

"Thank you, Dr. Phil," he says before clicking off the connection.

In chambers, the judge meets midmorning with John Banion to discuss his draft of an opinion in a preliminary injunction case the court took on an emergency appeal. It concerns a dispute between a theater chain and a movie distributor about box-office receipts and upcoming features.

"We need to toughen up the section on remedies," George tells his clerk. Banion sits before the judge's desk, nodding obediently. The contrast in character between George's two clerks could hardly be more striking. With five minutes' acquaintance, Cassie is likely to tell you the state of her dental work, the amount of her phone bill, and her pointed reflections on the many young men pursuing her.

John speaks very little, in a somewhat precious hush, and remains perpetually aloof.

Educated in Pennsylvania, John Banion returned here a decade ago to care for, then bury, his elderly parents. He is a highly capable lawyer, and for several years after the judge first hired him, he feared that Banion would give notice and move on to a better-paid job in private practice. But in George's lifetime that world has grown cruel to persons like John, able but uneasy with people and, thus, unlikely to charm clients. When George started out, those 'back room lawyers' were the foundation of large law firms. These days they are increasingly hired hands, who work crushing hours until they are replaced by younger versions of themselves. John is apparently content with his life here. He works from eight to five, earns enough, reads obsessively, and takes several trips each year to hike alone in wilderness areas.

Solitariness, however, is a motif. Since his parents' passing, John has slid into an increasingly reclusive and eccentric middle-aged bachelorhood. He retains a smooth, innocent face, but his brownish hair is departing quickly, and John has rounded noticeably in the last couple of years. Along the way, he seems to have lost most use for other people. It is routine to see him by himself in the courthouse cafeteria at lunch, his nose stuck in a book—usually a heavy philosophical tome—or pecking away on his laptop, while dozens of folks he has known for years and could easily join chat at tables nearby. John never mentions any social engagements, and the common assumption seems to be that he's gay. George, who does not regard himself as especially well attuned on that subject, still tends to doubt it. Aren't there genuine bachelors, unable to accommodate themselves to intimacy with anyone, who sink into the embrace of their own peculiarities?

But his oddness makes John in some ways a hero to his boss. The judge has often speculated that if he could put a probe in Banion's brain, he'd enter a world more colorful than some $200 million Hollywood epic. But John has found a bridge to the rest of the world in the law. He functions in the hermetic zone of the appellate court, as a valued professional. In George's judgment, John Banion is about as good as a law clerk gets. Precise. Talented. Unobtrusive.

"John," the judge says, as the clerk stands to have another go at the opinion, "Cassie tells me you don't mind if she does the drafts in *Warnovits*. I want to be certain she's not elbowing you out of the way."

"Hardly, Judge." He looks at the carpet and mutters, "If she wants to deal with all that stuff, let her. I've had enough of those boys." From John this is what passes as outspokenness. Generally, he embodies the selflessness to which the law aspires in the ideal. After nine years working with John, George still cannot tell whether he favors the prosecution or the defense, corporate interests or the little guy. He undertakes his work with the apparent disinterest of a shoemaker. Nonetheless, the judge has a brief, paralyzing thought of the comments Harry Oakey, Cassie's father and George's friend, might pass if he ever learned about his daughter's newest assignment, which will require her to study that videotape. Not the sort of education Harry had in mind when he sent his daughter to George's chambers.

The judge asks Banion to give Cassie the bench memos John prepared before the oral argument and to tell her she can start work.

"Still two drafts? Affirming and reversing?" John avoids a direct look, reluctant to confront the judge about his indecision, but it dawns on George that he is starting to make a fool of himself in his own chambers.

"It's a hard case, John. On the law. I seem to be stuck on the limitations issue. But whichever way I go, there will be a dissent. Koll wants the case reversed because the videotape couldn't be used, and Purfoyle's strictly for affirmance. I need to get my ducks in a row."

John departs, but with the discussion, George's thoughts drift back to *Warnovits*. The case, when he can bring himself to contemplate it, remains welded to his memories of Lolly Viccino. Eventually, as he kept her company in the dormitory library, he realized that her ragged look was due in part to having had no chance to bathe. Late in the afternoon, he stood guard outside the men's room so that Lolly could shower. It was there Grigson found him.

'She's still here?' Grigson asked.

George told the dorm proctor her story.

'Well. I'm very sorry to hear that, Mason, but if

her own people won't take her in, what are we to do? She can't stay.'

George stood the only ground he could. 'I'm not telling her.'

'Well, you don't have to,' Grigson said. 'You just move along, George Mason. I'll deal with this. Go on.' The dorm proctor waved the back of his hand. From the mettle that had come into him, George realized that the proctor had heard about the goings-on the night before. Franklin Grigson was going to enjoy turning out the likes of Lolly Viccino.

So, George thinks at his desk, he actually failed Lolly Viccino twice. He made no further protest on her behalf nor, more practically, did he escort her from the dorm to one of the local rooming houses, where he probably could have financed a leisurely stay for her after a frank chat with Hugh Brierly about the 'rent' he'd collected the night before. Instead, George did what kids do in tough situations — he hid. Visiting the library an hour later, he found the only remnant of Lolly's stay was the dirty plate from the canteen heaped with cigarette butts. George fingered one or two, overcome by things he could not explain. And yet he knew that, much as he had hoped the night before, some fundamental transition had begun for him.

For a second, George's guilt feels like a dagger point against his heart. How could he have made no effort to find out what had become of her? To see if she had even lived out the day safely? Or to determine what mark all this had left on her?

Banion knocks and returns from the small clerks' chambers with a draft of three new paragraphs to be inserted in the movie theater opinion.

"John, if I wanted to locate somebody I knew forty years ago in Virginia, is there any way to go about that?" His clerk can research anything on the Internet.

"What's the name, Your Honor?"

As soon as George gives it, he realizes this is an impossible task, even for John. Assuming the average course of events, she married and, as was usually the case with women from Virginia of his age, had given up Viccino. And Lolly could not have been the name on her birth certificate. Not to mention the fact that George has no idea of precisely where or when she was born. The judge shakes his head at length to show he's had second thoughts.

"It's a personal matter, John. Don't waste your time with this. I may poke around myself some evening. I just wondered how to go about it."

Banion has scratched out the names of a few Web sites on a pad, but the notion that the matter is personal is as good as crashing down a gate. John permits himself little, if any, inquiry into the lives of others and thus seems to have no clue how curious everyone is about him. This winter, he was down for days with a serious bronchial infection. Working from home, he had reluctantly asked Dineesha to bring him a set of briefs he needed. She is the one person in chambers with whom he holds any semblance of a personal relationship—they exchange small gifts at Christmas—but even she had never been to his house. When she returned, there was a palpable atmosphere of suspense. Cassie; the clerks from the adjoining chambers; Marcus, the elderly courtroom bailiff; and the judge himself—everyone awaited some description of what Dineesha had found. She was far too dignified to indulge them, but the next day, when she fetched in a messenger delivery, the judge said to her, 'Dare I ask?'

After gently closing the door, Dineesha rendered a brief but vivid portrait. The stucco bungalow, in which John's parents had raised him, had visible cracks in the outer walls and a patch of shingles missing from the roof. But the true bedlam was inside. It was not dirty, Dineesha said, but so dense with piles that she could barely get into the front hallway. It was as if he had a recycling center in the house. He did not appear to have thrown out a newspaper or magazine in the last ten years. They were piled in columns to the ceiling in the living room, where there was also a virtual fortification of books, in eight-foot ramparts as if to form a bunker. Under the load, the hardwood floor had literally begun to sag. Two parakeets flew free throughout the house and made a squeaking racket.

George is taken from these thoughts by a buzz arising somewhere in the room. The unfamiliar sound spooks him a bit until he realizes it's Patrice's cell groaning intermittently as it vibrates. Fishing it from the suit jacket that hangs behind him, the judge sees letters on the gray screen. A text message, his first ever. He's mildly pleased to have caught up with the times, until he reads what's there.

"Number One," he murmurs, "you are starting to get on my nerves." But he cannot kid himself. It's the first moment that requires a conscious effort to contain his fears. It's not so much the words—'Will get u'—that scare him. The threat is nothing new. What's frightening is the number from which the message comes. It's his, George's. Number one has the judge's missing cell phone.

11

TEMPER

At 3:00 P.M., Marina, who's been working with the phone company for several hours, arrives with one of her deputies, Nora Ortega, a thin, dark, silent woman whom Marina has brought along on a few occasions in the past to take notes. George makes it a point to offer Marina his hand, and she exerts her entire boxy form as she shakes.

"That was over the top, Judge, putting that tail on without telling you. Sorry."

He apologizes too, using the term 'grouchy old man.' They settle in familiar poses, George behind his desk, Marina in the black wooden armchair in front of it.

"So what did we learn about number 1?" he asks. "Anything good?"

"We've got some idea where he was. Which basically comes down to Center City."

They've assumed all along that George's tormentor is local, but this is the first proof. Nonetheless, the new information seems sparse compared with what he expected.

"I thought they could position a cell phone better than that."

"If it's turned on, Judge. But not if the phone is off. Which yours is, of course. It was probably off as soon as you got that text message."

"So how can they tell he was in Center City?"

"My guy over there wouldn't get very specific. They've got the government on one side and the ACLU on the other. He sort of explained all this by humming. But how I think this may go is that a cell phone actually puts out signals on two channels, and the company has a record of the second one, what's called control channel data, which includes the location of the cell your phone connects to. The best they can do is tell us that the message went through the tower in the steeple at St. Margaret's. He could have been anywhere within two square miles of there."

"So you've narrowed it down to about two hundred thousand suspects?"

"Exactly." Marina smiles. "We'll have them all interviewed by morning."

George is relieved that she has recovered her sense of humor with him. In the meantime, she holds up Patrice's spare cell phone, which she's brought back after getting all the info from it the telephone company needed.

"What I'm wondering is how he got this number."

"Because I was nice enough to give it to him," says George. "I was trying to find the phone I lost. So I called it. Made sense to me. When I got voice mail, I left a message. 'This is Judge George Mason. If you've picked up this cell phone, please call me at the following number.' I tried a few times."

"And how would he have gotten into your voice mail without your password?"

"The whole sequence is programmed into the

phone when you hold down the one key. Obviously he figured it out."

"Obviously," answers Marina.

"Any idea who else he called? Did he give himself up in some way?"

"Not really. The company says there's no detail in the last two weeks."

"Meaning?"

"If he used the phone, the calls are free under your plan. Voice mail. Stuff like that. He's smart," she says. "But we already knew that."

Next, she wants to replay how George's cell turned up missing and the steps his staff and he took to find it. After some talk, it makes more sense to include in the conversation everyone who had a role in the search, and George summons them. Dineesha and Cassie take places on the gray sofa beside Nora. Marcus, tall and bearded, stands at the door, working over a toothpick. Not to be overlooked, Abel wanders in last and with much effort puts himself down on a low colonial boot bench, next to John Banion.

George had noticed that the phone was not in his suit jacket pocket as he was leaving the Hotel

Gresham after the Kindle County Bar Association's Judges' Day event, two weeks ago yesterday, but his last clear recollection of having it went back to his departure from chambers the evening before. The staff and he attempted to retrace his steps over the intervening period. Banion called the hotel lost and found. Marcus checked to make sure George had not left it at the courthouse metal detectors that morning. Cassie phoned the restaurant where George had dinner the preceding night, and went out to search his car. Dineesha combed the chambers. The judge himself looked everywhere around his house when he returned there.

"Truth is, Marina, until today, I've been convinced I was going to lift some pile of papers and see it there." In the last few hours, fitting things together, George has been spinning another theory: Zeke took it. He now suspects that what Zeke was up to yesterday was an effort to lift something else. As George envisions the first episode, the road dog Khaleel must have walked up and down the corridor until he could see that everyone was out of chambers for a minute, then signaled Zeke, who came up and grabbed the phone. That way, if anyone returned and found Zeke inside, he could say he had just come by to visit. The judge is reluctant to try out this notion on Marina, however, until he's forewarned Dineesha. That's not a conversation he's looking forward to.

"Maybe I can help," says Marina. "According to the records the company pulled, your last charged call was the day you lost it at 12:12 P.M. One minute." She reads the number he'd dialed. It's Patrice's, her other cell.

"I must have been checking to see how she was," says the judge. "One minute means I probably got *her* voice mail." That's why he forgot making the call.

"And where were you?"

He cannot recollect. There have been so many stolen moments in so many corridors in the last months, brief, hushed conversations to let Patrice know she's on his mind.

"Do you remember when we left for the hotel?" George asks Cassie. He'd invited both clerks to the Judges' Day event, but John, as he does every year, had shunned the crowd.

Cassie searches her handheld.

"We were supposed to meet the other judges in the lobby at 11:45. We were out of here by five till, for sure." The Chief insists on punctuality in all things. All but two or three of the judges of the appellate court, a dozen and a half of them, and their clerks had been transported by Marina's staff to the hotel in several vans. George and Cassie both recall being in the first vehicle to leave.

"So you called from the hotel, Your Honor?"

He seems to remember that now. Had he stood just outside the men's room? Cassie recollects the judge going off for a few minutes before they entered the reception. But a vague memory is so suggestible. Neither Cassie nor he had put this together the day after. Perhaps #1 had the phone in hand at 12:12 and had hit the speed-dial keys to see where they would take him. But why just one? Thinking now, the judge is fairly certain he'd clicked off the connection when he got Patrice's voice message.

"Best recollection," he answers, a lawyer's phrase that passes for truth in the courtroom.

"Meaning he picked your pocket there," Marina says.

"That doesn't do much for your Corazón theory, does it?" George says to her. There's no point in shying away from the name after Marina broke silence yesterday. After a second, the judge realizes that Zeke has also become a far less likely suspect, assuming the phone was lifted at the hotel.

"I don't see that."

"Come on, Marina. You think a kid in baggies and a prison buzz is going to walk into the Kindle County Bar meeting, with two hundred judges and six hundred lawyers around, and stick his hand in my suit jacket?"

"Judge, you know what goes on with the gangs these days. Cops are undercover, and so are they. Do you really believe, Your Honor, that if we did a background on the servers, and the security guards, and the people taking coats we wouldn't find one person with a connect to ALN? A quarter of the guards in the jail are courted in, Judge. Hell, not to be repeated, but there are a couple of people on my staff that Gang Crimes has questions about. If Corazón wanted to boost your cell, he could find somebody to do it."

Empiricism will never guide police work. Investigators fashion their theories and shape all evidence to fit. Forget the hatreds between the black and Latin gangs, the near impossibility of picking out George as a mark in a crowd of eight hundred. Corazón's still the man. There are moments when George cannot avoid falling back into the grip of the perpetual antagonism he felt as a defense lawyer toward the cops and the way their habits shortcut the truth. And in this he reaches the hard rock of what's between Marina and him: she's more or less insisting he run scared.

"May I be blunt?" the judge asks her.

She takes a beat. "Sure."

"Maybe you ought to ask yourself, Marina, what it's worth to you to stick to Corazón."

"'Worth'?"

"I use the term advisedly. How much do you get to add to your emergency funding request to the County Board when you can trot out a name like Corazón's? Ten percent? Twenty percent?"

Marina sucks her cheeks into her mouth.

"Whoa," she says and glances over her shoulder

SCOTT TUROW

to observe Nora's reactions. "Judge, I think you're
starting to forget who's on your side."

When George Mason reaches home that night, he
finds Patrice asleep in their room and steals back
downstairs to the large kitchen she designed several
years ago. There's a profusion of light from a rectangular walnut-and-glass fixture. The cabinets match,
with panes of German crackle glass inset with rectangular rose-color panels, all the elements intended
to complement the existing fireplace in what was
the living room when they bought. The space has a
mellow warmth, and it's probably his favorite place
in the house, but tonight it cannot alter his mood.
Solitude only allows him to wallow. He's yet to
recover from his second dustup with Marina. It's a
point of pride that he seldom loses his temper, and
justified or not, it was thoughtless to blast her in
front of everyone. Worst of all was the look on her
face. George knows enough at this age to realize
that somebody who followed her father into his
profession is going to be especially vulnerable to the
opinion of older men. She left with a chafed,

sorrowful expression, which might as well have been an ice pick in George's heart.

Then at the end of the day, Cassie gave the judge outlines of the two potential opinions in *Warnovits* in the hope he would look at them over the weekend and choose between them. Examining the pages on the slate-topped kitchen island pulls him down further. Both drafts make sense, naturally. There's no analytic trick he learned in law school or since then that allows him to pick one or the other apart. For a century and a half, legal education has been focused on reading the opinions of judges like George who sit on courts of review. In his day, his professors discussed these decisions, just as they would now, in terms of the policy concerns, the political views, the jurisprudential beliefs that drove them. After holding this job for nearly a decade, he regards much of what he was taught as romantic, if not completely wrong.

Most of the time, no matter what your political or philosophical stripes, whether you like the law or not, you find that your decision feels preordained. Even when you can imagine a route to another result, loyalty to the institution of the law, and more particularly to other judges, good women and men who've sat where you sit and who've done their level best to decide similar cases, requires you to follow the same paths they've trod. The discretion his professors talked about exists only on the margins, in no better than three or four cases a term.

But *Warnovits* is one of them, where neither the words of the legislature nor prior decisions will yield a sure answer. Ugly as the crime was, these boys were prosecuted later than the law normally allows. The trial judge—Farrell Kirk, no Cardozo but a reasonable guy—made a fair reading of the conceal-ment provision and a balanced assessment of the testimony, and Sapperstein is equally right that, in doing so, Kirk basically erased the neat boundaries the legislators had drawn on how long a victim's age could lawfully prolong the time to indictment. With the arguments essentially even, the truth is that the law in this case will be whatever George Mason says it is. And right now the best he can do is flip a coin. He actually removes a quarter from his pocket and sets it on the counter beside the drafts. Even to Patrice, he has never admitted that in the last nine and a half years he has decided two cases this way, albeit tiny civil matters in which the decisional law was a hopeless mess.

He is still staring at the coin when Patrice wanders in, drawing her hands down her face to drain off the sleep. By reflex, she moves forward to kiss him in greeting, then thinks better of that. She'll be minimally radioactive until early Sunday.

"Wow," she says, focusing on him. "What did the bartender say when the horse came into the tavern?"

He smiles wanly at the old joke: Why the long face?

"Nay," he says, "nay, not that one."

He gets a simpering grin before Patrice goes to the fridge for a bottle of water. Her back is still to him when he asks, "What would you say if I didn't run for retention?"

"What?"

"I've actually been thinking about it. I could work less and make twice as much money. We could travel."

She has finally completed her slow turn.

"George, you love this job. You've always loved

this job. How can you even possibly consider that? What's changed?"

He lifts his hands. She watches him without much charity. If he has one lasting lament in their marriage, it's the way Patrice can go cold at the core. Her father, Hugo Levi, was a morose son of a bitch, a lawyer by training who went into the packaging business. He had his own sad history—a mother dead before he was five—but he punished his family by often growing stonily remote and in those moods voicing heartless judgments. Having come of age in the Old South, George has probably fought no biblical notion harder than the idea that the sins of the father are destined to be punished for generations. He despised the suggestion that a free human being should simply yield to fate and, worse, the idea that he could not be freed from the effects of what he despised. But he's at an age when he's come to recognize the scripture's wisdom. Patrice yearned for the embrace of this hard man and in so doing took a slice of him into herself. She's never had a gentle way of expressing her disappointments. And she's clearly disappointed now.

"Look, mate." She leans over the counter so she

is beside him, closer than she's been for days. "I want to say something to you. I've tried not to, but you have to hear this: Stop being scared. I can see it on you, George. You're scared. And it bothers the hell out of me. I look at you, and I think, What have the doctors told him they haven't told me? You're making this a lot worse than it has to be. It's hard enough to handle myself. I can't handle you too. You can have your eleventh midlife crisis on your own time. But it's my time now."

"Patrice—"

His wife leaves the kitchen, looking back to speak just one word more: "No."

12

GETTING THE MESSAGE

George has been at his desk for only a few minutes on Monday morning when Dineesha enters from the reception area. She leaves the door ajar, addressing the judge in formal timbre.

"Your Honor, Judge Koll was hoping you might have a minute for him. He's right outside."

"Crap," George mouths. Nine A.M. and Nathan has already come to demand the draft of the *Warnovits* opinion. He can't bear to wait any longer to see the target he'll be shooting at in his dissent.

"Nathan!" George cries, hail fellow well met, as he strides out.

On the green sofa beside Abel Birtz, Koll is drawn into himself like a molting bird, his dark face screwed up in a stormy look. He's come down without his suit coat, and his white shirt looks as if it should have seen the laundry three wearings ago, wrinkled like a discarded lunch bag.

"I need to speak with you," he says and charges past George into his inner chambers. "Look at this!" He reaches into his shirt pocket. "Look at this, for Chrissake."

Nathan has withdrawn an envelope, from which he next removes a single sheet, the lower half stained brown.

"It was in the morning mail."

After the first glance, George places the paper on his desk to avoid handling it further. It's a printout of one of the bounced e-mails George received: "You'll bleed." That, George realizes, accounts for the irregular blot on the bottom half. Dried blood.

"Have you contacted Marina, Nathan?"

"Well, I thought I'd give you a chance to explain,

George. I can't imagine what you were doing sending that kind of message to anyone."

George calls out to Dineesha to summon Court Security, then explains the situation to Koll.

"Oh my God," he says several times. "You must be jumping out of your skin. I heard there was something unsettling going on. I had no idea it had reached this level."

"'Heard something,' Nathan?"

"You know the clerks gossip. One of them mentioned that you'd been getting annoying e-mails. I thought that meant spam. Not death threats. Good Lord! No wonder you're hesitant to run again."

In other circumstances, George might take the last remark as tactical, designed to smoke out his intentions, but Koll looks completely unstrung. He's slumped in one of the wooden chairs in front of George's desk, and there's a rill of sweat next to his overgrown sideburn. What could be harder on a paranoid than real enemies? Because it's Koll, George cannot shutter a ray of competitive joy. Even in his worst instants, he hasn't been this frightened. Not yet.

"Frankly, Nathan, I think it's all hot air."

"And why's that?"

George's reasoning that a real assault would not come with so many warnings does nothing to comfort Koll.

"You're trying to mind-read a lunatic." He twists about in the chair, too agitated to find a comfortable position. "But why am I part of this now? That's what I'm trying to figure out." Being himself, Nathan shows no reluctance about wishing upon George solitary misfortune. "Is it our rape case? All the publicity about it?"

That makes no sense to either judge when they discuss it. Their decision in *Warnovits* is unknown, even to them, let alone to the passionate partisans on both sides of the case. And George was getting these e-mails long before the oral argument, which was the first occasion their roles in the case became public. The identities of the judges on the panels are among the court's more closely guarded secrets in order to prevent lawyers from basing their oral arguments on the prior opinions of the sitting judges instead of relying on the larger body of court precedents.

"I thought *Warnovits* was why you were here,

Nathan. To get my draft. I'm going to need a few more days. Frankly, I'm trying to figure out how to come up with a real majority. We can't send this thing out into the world with three judges saying three different things. I've been giving some thought to joining you and letting your draft on the inadmissibility of the tape become the opinion for the court."

In practical terms, this resolution has many virtues, springing from the scenario Rusty played out last week. Some of the young defendants—perhaps all but Warnovits—would plea-bargain to eavesdropping in exchange for their testimony about the rape. They would end up with lighter sentences than the minimum-mandatory six years imposed for the sexual assault, which is a suitable outcome in George's mind, given the otherwise admirable lives the young men have led. The truth is that the limitations issue made this an ideal case for a compromise, which should have been struck long ago. But somehow reason had faltered, due perhaps to the prosecutors' inflexibility, or the ego of defense counsel, or the unwillingness of the young men or their parents to accept the inevitability of prison. From the Olympian height of the appellate court, there is never any telling why a deal was not reached, because the negotiations are rarely a matter of record. Yet the result of the failure to resolve the case is clear: the courts were left with only stark choices.

But no matter how tempting it is to play Solomon after the fact, George remains roadblocked by the law. He still cannot call the verdict or sentences a wholesale miscarriage of justice, even if the punishment for some of the young men is more severe than what he'd impose. After thirty-plus years in the legal system, George has accepted that "justice" is no better than approximate, a range of tolerable results.

Instead, he has tossed out the idea of using Koll's opinion largely to test Rusty's suspicions of Nathan. George is curious to see if Koll exhibits any reluctance to replace him as the principal target of the public wrath that will surely await the author of an opinion reversing these convictions. And the Chief, it develops, may have been right.

"Yes, I've been thinking about the same problem," Koll says. "Three opinions. Something has to give. Perhaps I'll concur on the statute of limitations, so you can speak for the majority. Then I'll write separately about the videotape. Let me see your draft when you're done. And I'll e-mail mine. It's finished."

Naturally. George cannot quite contain a smile. What vain illusion made him think Nathan would wait until he'd seen what George had to say before disagreeing with it? Hearing Dineesha greeting Murph, Marina's deputy chief, out in the reception area, George stands.

"By the way, Nathan. Don't read too much into the fact that I haven't filed my retention petition."

"Oh?"

"I've been waiting for the last little concerns about Patrice's condition to be cleared up. But she couldn't possibly be doing better."

"Oh." Koll cannot keep his jaw from going limp. About to rise from his chair, he loses his momentum. Even with his angst about the threat from #1, this may be the worst news to come to his way today.

Over the weekend, George gave himself the break he had needed. He woke up Saturday morning knowing Patrice and he had to cross the breach and insisted that they drive up to their cabin in Skageon. The hell with what the doctors would advise; he'd read enough on his own to know that after five days the risks to him were picayune.

It was the right idea. The weather was glorious. They walked, made dinner together, drank a bottle of Corton-Charlemagne, and were finally together in the same bed. It was just as it was thirty years before, when the extraordinary sensations of sleeping beside someone after a lifetime alone made the night one long embrace. This reunion, and the longings it satisfied, was a tribute to their mutual well-being.

But vacations end, and Koll's visit has brought with it the dismal knot of feelings that has long accompanied *People v. Warnovits*. The judge spends a meditative instant seeing if he is ready to decide the case, with the same stillborn results. He continues to sit first in judgment of himself, and that process remains incomplete. The idle notion of trying to find Lolly Viccino, which he briefly raised with Banion last week, continues to attract him, although he cannot say why. What comfort does he think she could give him forty years after the fact? He can hardly expect her to say it had all been okay. The best to hope for is that she, much as he did, was able to put away the incident by dismissing it as part of the temporary psychosis called youth. But still he lets his imagination roll out for a second. What might have become of Lolly?

Just as with the telephone, George normally does nothing but official business on the computer in his chambers: he will not read personal e-mail or order theater tickets there. But it's clear now, he'll never decide *Warnovits* until he's more resolved about what happened in Virginia long ago.

'Lolly Viccino' brings no results from any of the search engines. As a best guess about her given name, George decides to try again with 'Linda.'

An hour and a half later, he has isolated three possibilities. In Scotland, a Linda Viccino works as a safety inspection teacher. The information on the Web site of the regional electric authority is cryptic, but it appears that Linda Viccino instructs other government officials on how to examine power plants for dangerous conditions. Contemplating this life for a second, he deems it a relatively happy ending for Lolly. She has gotten an education, a responsible job. She has left her unhappy home far behind. What took her overseas? Love, George hopes. That was the story with most of his friends from college or law school who ended up as expats—they met someone and chose romance over America. It would be nice if that was what happened to Lolly too.

The second Linda Viccino turns up as a hundred-dollar donor to the Children's Trust Fund for the Prevention of Child Abuse in Mississippi. It's pleasing to think of Lolly as a generous adult, but the mission of the charity is vaguely troubling. Perhaps she's a mom, who naturally recoils at the thought of kids being treated that way. Or does she regard herself as a formerly abused child—and George, and all those other young men whom she met in that cardboard hothouse, as having continued the pattern?

The third Linda Viccino represents the most disquieting prospect. Her name appears in cemetery records in Massachusetts, not far from Boston. 'Linda Viccino 1945–70.' This woman might have been born a year or two too soon to have been

Lolly, but he considers the possibility. What kills a person at twenty-five? Leukemia. An accident. But George knows the better odds are that someone who passes at that age dies of unhappiness. Drug overdose. Suicide. Reckless behavior. In this version of Lolly, there was no escape for the young woman who had declared, 'My life stinks, you can't believe how much my life stinks.'

He has finally given up his research and gone on to other work when Koll's draft dissent in *Warnovits* pops up in George's e-mail. It's Koll's usual bravura performance, trampling like a marching army over opposing ideas. George finds himself amused by the contrast between the bold legal conquistador and the man who sat here unraveled by #1. It's not news, however, that Nathan's paranoia compels an element of physical cowardice. The second or third time George sat with him, Koll retreated into silence, plainly intimidated by the reputation of the defendant.

Trying to draw back the particulars of the case, George ultimately goes still when his memory solidifies. He remembers now. *People v. Jaime Colon.*

The appellant who terrified Nathan was Corazón.

13

CORAZÓN'S HAND

Court security is relegated to a cramped office off the main lobby, a warren of filing cabinets and fabric workstation dividers. The lower floors of the Central Branch building never received any of the deluxe refurbishing that went on upstairs to make way for the appellate court. The half-height oak tongue-in-groove paneling on the plaster walls has the yellowish cast of its decades-old varnish, and the tall double-hung windows are rattling antiques. When he asks for Marina, one of her clerical workers, all 'suggested' for her payroll by members of the

County Board, points over his head to her office without glancing up from a computer screen.

Marina is on the phone, and the look that stiffens her rectangular face when she takes notice of the judge tells the whole story. Bygones are not gone yet.

"Later," she says into the handset. Pictures of Marina's sisters and their families, of her parents, and of a woman, a deputy U.S. marshal, whom Marina took to the court's holiday party last year, are arrayed in matching gold frames on her desk. "Judge," she says neutrally as she puts down the phone.

"So," George says, taking the seat she has offered, "I just wanted you to know that when I left here on Friday I went home and had a fight with my wife too. But," he adds, "I did not kick the dog."

She nods.

"Then again, we don't own a dog."

He gets the smile he wanted. "It's a lot of stress, Judge. I wouldn't trade places with you."

"Just to be said, Marina: I'm grateful for everything you've done. I know you're trying to save my scaly hide."

She beams like a little kid, but it's brief. She's reluctant to be charmed.

"Your Honor, I have to be frank. The biggest problem I've got in this whole situation is getting you to take it seriously. Even if it's one in ten that I'm right, you can't act as if the chances are zero. Can you maybe ask yourself if you're in denial?"

"Point taken," he answers. "And actually, that's why I'm here. I just realized that Nathan Koll sat on the panel with me when we heard Corazón's appeal."

"Oh, yeah," she answers. "Koll went nuclear when Murph mentioned the name. The judge would just as soon we go down to the supermax and poison Corazón's food." Marina draws her cheeks in to contain her expression, but she has to feel like a kindergarten teacher at times, having to indulge the judges and their mercurial demands. "Tell me something," she says. "Judge Koll—he's a smart guy, isn't he?"

"Just ask him."

"Yeah, right. How does somebody who's supposed to be so brilliant grab that message with both hands about two hundred times? The only prints of value are his—and there were so many overlapping impressions we couldn't even isolate most of them. I know number 1 probably used latex gloves, but jeez Louise, give us a chance."

"He seemed pretty scared, Marina."

"I guess. But you should have heard him squawk about getting printed. What did he expect after that?"

George can only imagine how many of Nathan's phobias were activated by having his hands inked and pressed onto the cards. He must have lit up like a pinball machine.

"That's beef blood on the paper, by the way," Marina says. "Guess Corazón learned his lesson about DNA." She kicks back and perches a short leg, in the piped khaki trousers of her uniform, over an open desk drawer. "So you're liking Corazón now?"

"More. But do I get to tell the truth?"

"Today's the last time," she says.

"My divining rod still isn't rattling on Corazón. Did you follow up on Zeke, Dineesha's son?"

"Best we could. Couple Kindle dicks made several home visits on Friday hoping to spend a little quality time with him. Turns out Zeke was in St. Louis. He's got a new gig, in-store marketing for one of the cell phone companies. Says he did so good they made him one of the trainers. He does these day-and-a-half sessions Fridays and Saturday until noon."

"Cell phones, huh?"

"Yeah," she says. "I had the same thought. But he had his boarding passes, hotel bill, expense report, training manuals."

"Coppers believed him?"

"About that? Pretty much. Can't get on an airplane without a photo ID, Judge. I mean, he was in St. Louis."

Of course, Zeke could have had someone else, like his road dog Khaleel, text George from the stolen phone, realizing that a day when he was alibied made the perfect occasion for more hijinks. That's the way the cops would think about it, and that's exactly what Marina says.

"Overall, though," she adds, "they don't think Zeke is our guy. But a couple things bothered the two that were talking with him. First off, Zeke knew why they were there. This big indignant routine that anybody would think he might do you wrong after all the help you've given him."

That's the right line. But Zeke's a capital liar, tied for the title of the best George has ever seen along with dozens of other former clients—and several attorneys.

"Need I ask how he knew the police were coming?"

"I don't think so." Marina crumples her chin in a hard-bitten smile. "And he was still sticking to that shit about needing the john when they pressed about why his buddy was cruising your corridor. But"—she shrugs—"he wasn't the one who sent out that text, and he didn't mail that letter to Koll either. Postmark is 'Pueblocito' Saturday morning." She's referring to the Tri-Cities' largest Hispanic neighborhood, in Kewahnee, where Corazón's set thrives. "That's a lot for Zeke to put together from out of town. Corazón, Judge. That's the better bet."

George shakes his head just a little, trying not to be irksome.

"This letter doesn't feel right to me, Marina. I've been getting e-mails for weeks. Why put Koll into it suddenly? Especially when it draws a line straight to Corazón?"

"That's Corazón, Judge. Why does a guy go out himself and beat up a woman and two babies with a tire iron when he can send three hundred other cholos to do it? 'Cause he's the fearless, fucking Corazón. He sticks out his you-know-what and says 'Do me something,' and laughs himself to sleep when you can't. That's how he gets off."

George considers the point. "But up until now, number 1 has been kind of a high-tech pain in the ass. Very smooth, very clever. A bloodstained piece of paper comes out of a 1950s horror movie."

"Worked on Judge Koll."

"So would an e-mail."

"I don't know, Your Honor. Corazón had a visit with Mom two days before that letter flew."

"Monitored, though. Right?"

"Sure. But hell, Judge, when they start yapping about Tío Jorge in Durango, what do we know? That could be code for anything. But let me hear it, Judge. What are you thinking?"

"Maybe a copycat? Maybe somebody who's got an ax to grind with Nathan and took a free shot."

She shrugs once more, doing her best to seem open to the possibility.

"My old man always says you solve crimes with the KISS rule," she says. "You know that one?"

He does, but he lets her say it for the sake of amity.

"Keep It Simple, Stupid."

Back at his desk, George works until close to 6:30. Patrice returned to the office today and expects to be late, moving through the mountains on her desk, but Abel is pawing around out in the reception area, peeking in now and then. This duty keeps him well past his customary hour of departure. George had hoped to edit two more draft opinions, but he throws them in his briefcase. He'll look them over at home tonight.

"All right, Abel," he calls, "saddle up."

Together they make their slow progress across the gangway into the judges' section of the garage, Abel swinging his leg around his arthritic hip. As they approach the entrance, the two boys George saw last week are lurking once more. Their hairstyles mark them as gang members. The taller one has a do called a patch, close-cropped over his ears but grown long on the back of his scalp, borrowed, it seems, from American Indians. The other has a standard prison buzz. Despite the warm weather, both are clad again in hooded sweatshirts.

Abel stares them down. "Don't like the looks of those two," he says. "What are they up to?"

"Waiting for a ride home?"

"Yeah," Abel says, "in the car they're gonna jack. They ain't countin' their rosary beads, Judge. Let's get 'em on their way." He reaches for the radio on his belt to alert the dog patrol.

That's the course of wisdom. In some moods, George might even call Court Security himself. On average, you could not go wrong thinking the worst about most of the young men you saw around this building. The best bet is that the two are baby Gs, gang wannabes not fully courted in, who are here to hold on to guns or dope so senior set members can pass through the metal detectors on their way to afternoon drug court.

But George has always discouraged himself from taking those kinds of probabilities as the actual truth. The real George Mason was the source of the phrase, appropriated by his pal Jefferson, 'All men are created equal.' The sentiments were noble, but George Mason IV was a slave owner notwithstanding, just like nearly every one of George's Virginia ancestors. It is the most shameful of the many unhappy legacies George fled in his twenties, and he came here determined to be a man of more open inclinations. Throughout his life, he has made a disciplined effort to take human beings one at a time.

"Leave them be, Abel. They're not hurting anybody." After his fight with Patrice on Friday night, he also feels duty-bound to resist the creeping fears inspired by #1. Better to be bold. "I saw them here a couple times last week. They didn't seem to make any trouble."

As if it were a date, Abel escorts George all the way to the car. The judge triggers the engine and turns on the air, watching the old guy recede. George is not ready to go yet. As usual, he wants a minute to himself, in this case to think about the three lives of Lolly Viccino he was envisioning a few hours ago at his desk. He reclines in the cushy car seat, eyes closed. At the moment, it's the second

Lolly who preoccupies him, the contributor to the Mississippi child abuse fund. She has to be all right, someone with a stake in the community and the future. He imagines a Mississippi lady in a long pink dress, wearing a hat and gloves, but laughs at the notion. That would never be Lolly.

George is trying to reconfigure his vision of her when he is startled by a sharp rap beside him. He snaps up and sees two things: the silver barrel of an automatic lying solidly against the glass, and the five-pointed star of the Almighty Latin Nation tattooed below the wrist of the hand that holds the gun.

14

A VICTIM

Outside the window, the gun muzzle, a spot of total blackness, looms a few inches from the judge's face. George notices eventually that the boy is motioning with the other hand, but he has no clue what the kid wants, and the young man bangs the pistol on the glass again in rebuke. This is how people get shot, George thinks. By failing to follow orders they don't comprehend. And then, remembering Corazón, he realizes that he is going to get shot anyway.

That thought pumps the harshest adrenaline rush yet through him. Inside his head there is a chaos of colliding ideas, each one as urgent as a scream.

For all the years George has spent on the periphery of crime, he has never been on the receiving end of any violence. Everything he knows is second-hand from contemplating victims across the clinical distances of courtrooms, where he has tried to assess their credibility and, in his years as a lawyer, shake their stories. At trial, the suffering of the vics is often minimized; it's irrelevant to proving whether a crime occurred or who committed it. They rarely get to say much more about what they felt than 'I was afraid I was going to die.' And oddly, in this instant, George sees the wisdom of that. Language, rules, and reason can never capture this moment; they are definitional only by their absence, just as absolute zero is the complete absence of heat.

The boy's free hand circles through the air again. At last, George realizes the kid wants him to lower the driver's-side window, and he presses the button. But as the glass slides into the door, a faint outcry stirs inside him. It's like slipping off his skin. He was already at the boy's mercy, but with the last vestige of privacy gone, he knows he's on the way to surrendering his soul.

"'Kay now, *puto*," the boy says. "Give it up, man." 'Men' it sounds like in the boy's trace accent.

In his years as a State Defender, George cross-examined countless victims in armed-robbery cases. You always challenged the identification of the defendant the same way. By pointing out the obvious. 'And you were watching that gun, weren't you, Mrs. Jones? You never took your eyes off it, did you?' And it's true. He has not yet dared to raise his sight line. He has seen little more than the pistol, a small silver automatic, with a higher-caliber bore and black grips, and the hand that holds it, where the blue-black star of the Latin Nation is imprinted on the tan flesh just beneath the frayed gray sleeve of the boy's sweatshirt.

But when the kid speaks, George looks up compliantly. He already knows the boy is one of the two they saw on the way into the garage whom Abel wanted to roust. This is the taller kid, with that patch hairdo that always reminds George of a shaved radish. Now it is hidden under the hood of his sweatshirt, which is drawn around his face, the better to prevent identification. He's lanky and cannot be seventeen yet, with dark, bumpy skin and jittery eyes. Mexican or Central American. He has the high cheekbones and aquiline nose of native blood. Seeing the two boys from a distance over the last week, George marked them from their unchanged, ratty clothes as poor—really poor, locked-in poor, kids who rarely have the means to get beyond the barrio. It would be a miracle if this kid has ever had a conversation longer than a minute with an Anglo in a two-piece suit.

And realizing that he is largely incomprehensible to this boy, George considers what his chances will be if he puts the car in gear and tears away. Will the kid be too surprised to shoot? The idea comes, and he reacts to it. Some intermediate mental process has been evaporated by fear. George's hand slides to the gearshift, and instantly the boy slams the gun down solidly on his forearm. The pain is intense, but George knows better than to cry out. It's the boy who makes all the noise.

"*Fuck, puto!*" he cries. "Fuck, man, you gonna get yourself so pealed, man. What's up with you?

Fuck," the kid says and in pure frustration slams the pistol backhand again on the same arm, which the judge has withdrawn toward his chest. This time a cry escapes George, and he lies against the seat with his eyes closed for a second, contending with the pain.

The boy is snapping his fingers.

"Give 'em here, *puto.* Right here, man." He's demanding the car key. George's right arm is too numb to move. He turns in his seat and slides the key from the ignition with his left hand.

"Now give it up, man," the boy repeats, circling the gun again. He wants George out of the car. They are not going to kill him here, George realizes. They are going to take him somewhere else, because they're afraid the gunfire will attract the dog patrol before they can escape.

The boy again tells him to give it up. George continues to rub his arm, acting as if he's too preoccupied with the pain to listen. He considers various speeches: 'I'm a judge.' 'You don't understand how much trouble you'll get yourselves in.' But they might well make it worse. The last thing he needs to do is add incentives. To this young man, George's killing is almost certainly a gang initiation, 'blood in,' as they say. Corazón would have kicked the job down several levels, so that the judge's murder, a capital offense, will never trace to him. For a second, George considers Marina and Abel, both justified in all of their suspicions. They will be entitled to a moment of pained laughter at his expense. But George is pleased to discover that he doesn't mind. He knew he was taking his chances. Principle always comes with certain risks.

This instant of minute satisfaction ends when the boy punches the gun barrel into the judge's temple to reacquire his attention. George recoils, and the kid grabs his shoulders and prods his neck with the muzzle. He can feel his pulse in the artery the cool steel is pressing against.

"Yo, *vato*," somebody else says.

Afraid to remove his head from the pistol, George sweeps his eyes as far he can toward the passenger's side of his sedan. The second kid he saw earlier is at the other door. He's nearly a foot shorter than the boy holding the gun on George and younger. His arms are at his sides, but from the sheer drag on the right, George senses that he's holding a firearm, too. The second boy rotates his chin.

At the far corner of the garage someone else has entered from the opposite stairwell. Without moving, George catches a glimpse of dark clothes. He was hoping to see the khaki of Marina's security forces, but it's only somebody like him, another late departure from the courthouse, probably a deputy P.A. or State Defender working on a trial. The footfalls are a woman's, her high heels rapping smartly on the concrete. George listens before concluding disconsolately that the sound is moving away.

Scream, he tells himself. He has previewed this situation a thousand times through his career, looking up from a transcript or a police report and coldly assessing the victim's options. If they are going to kill him but are reluctant to do it here, then screaming is the best choice. The boy with the automatic at George's throat will be put to a decision. To run. Or shoot. Running would give him the best chance to get away. But George senses that he has exhausted the kid's patience. He tried to escape once. Respect, the credo of the street, is likely to be the foremost issue. And there's another problem. The judge is not really sure he can summon the voice for anything better than a meek croak.

George has always known you can be so frightened it hurts. His right forearm is throbbing, and his temple is tender, but there's also pain throughout his body. His muscles have spasmed below his armpits for some reason. And he's damp inside his shirt.

The boy has hunched down beside the Lexus while keeping the handgun against the base of the judge's skull. An engine fires several rows over, and a car pulls away. As it rolls off, George feels a wave of despair. It was a mistake, he decides. He should have shouted.

"Give it up, man," the kid says again.

George shakes his head.

"Yo, *puto*. Get your fuckin' ass out here, man, or it's comin' right through this damn window." The boy reaches in and takes hold of George's necktie. He gives it a sharp jerk, smashing the judge's cheek against the door frame, but he does not wait to see if George has changed his mind about cooperating.

The kid does exactly as promised, using the tie as a leash and pulling George out the open driver's window. Instinctively, George grabs for the seat belt hanging inside the door, but it pays out as the boy drags George's entire upper body into the outer air. He is left gasping, with both hands at his collar. In whatever hissing voice he can muster, he has said 'Okay' a dozen times before the boy finally eases his grip.

The kid slowly backs off from the door and watches George emerge. The other boy bounds to this side of the car now, waiting at its rear. George was right. He too has a gun.

Standing, George feels his legs wobbling. He is afraid he's going to topple, and he begs himself not to fall over, not so much out of pride as a sense that it will only enhance the danger.

"Wallet," the kid says. He takes George's watch too, and his class ring from college, then makes George turn out every pocket in his suit and surrender the contents. After that, the two boys motion George away from his car. He backs off about ten feet, still rubbing his forearm. He has no idea what is happening and wonders if they are going to shoot him here after all, but that makes no sense. If they were going to do that, it would have happened by now.

Instead, the first boy slides through the opened car door into the driver's seat and triggers the engine. He nods to his companion, who has been holding his black gun, probably a .32, on the judge in the interval.

Please, God, not the trunk, George thinks then. They are going to force him into the car. Not the trunk. And with that, he realizes he's going to stand his ground. They can choke him here, or pistol-whip him, but he's not going to submit. He'll scream if he has to. The end, whatever it will be, is going to take place on this spot.

His soul has compressed around that decision when he hears the second boy scampering away. He flees around the Lexus and into the passenger's seat, and the kid driving throws the car into reverse. George realizes too late that he had a brief chance to run. Having backed the sedan out, the boy looks through the open window at George, who stands no more than two or three feet from him. The judge is not surprised at all when the silver gun reappears.

Shoot and drive, he thinks. That's the plan. Kill him and escape. He had it wrong. All wrong.

"*Puto*," the boy says, "you ask Jesus tonight, man, why it wasn't shovel time for you. I should have lit you up, man, pulling that lame stuff. Ought to make you kiss this *cuete*," he says, showing him the automatic.

It takes George a second to absorb these words, and even longer to comprehend the implications. And then he sees: They are not going to kill him. They never meant to kill him. This is a robbery, not a murder. They are here to jack him and his car.

For whatever reason, the boy is still staring, as if he expects George to explain, or even offer a word of thanks. And somehow he agrees.

"I thought you were someone else," he tells the boy. They are both astonished by that—George that he has spoken and the kid by what the older man has said. The kid's dark, quick eyes move around in bewilderment.

"Man," he declares, and with that stomps on the accelerator. The Lexus, George's private refuge, flies around a turn and out of sight.

He looks for something to sit on, but the closest

thing is one of the concrete pillars, and he leans against it, waiting for the feeling to come back into his body. For a moment, he does nothing but breathe, each inhalation a supreme experience. In relief, he is weakening. His legs are overcooked, and slowly he lets his weight go and sags with his back against the pillar down to the filthy, oil-stained floor. He tries to review the entire incident, but there is only one lasting impression. He was wrong. Everything he thought was wrong. He has always believed he understood crime, the causes, the preparation, and the aftermath. But it turns out that, in thirty years, he has apparently learned nothing of any real use. Or accuracy. He misapprehended everything, resisted unnecessarily, and by so doing brought himself into the only mortal peril he actually faced.

Slowly his spirit seems to be creeping back into his body from the site nearby where it had been watching, preparing for his demise. Every physical possession is gone. He handed over not only his wallet but his house keys, even his reading glasses and his loose change. He does not have Patrice's cell phone but can't recall giving that to the boy and wonders if he may have left it in his chambers.

He never really understood, he thinks. He never fully comprehended. That in the end, or at the start, a human being is only this: a single humiliated fiber that wants desperately to live. He considers the messages he has been receiving and the foolhardy bravery he has tried to display. All pointless. At the moment of consequence, nothing matters but staying alive.

Patrice could have told him that. It was what she must have experienced when the doctor prodded beneath her larynx and said he didn't care for what he felt. And so George Mason sits there on the gritty floor, thinking with regret and admiration about his wife.

15

SURVIVING

Getting back into the courthouse seems to take forever. He bangs on the glass of the front door with his one good hand for at least five minutes, and when the night security officer, another useless member of Marina's khaki tribe, finally ambles to the window, he winds his head like something on a spring.

"Court's closed," the khaki officer mouths before turning his back. He probably takes George for a lawyer who missed the filing deadline on an appellate brief he hopes to slip through the mail slot of the clerk's office.

"I'm a judge!" George keeps screaming. "I've been assaulted." Eventually, Joanna Dozier, a deputy P.A. who is working late, recognizes him, and the police, at last, are summoned.

Awaiting the cops, George goes up to his chambers. He removes an ice tray from the freezer compartment in the tiny refrigerator in the corner and applies it to his shirtsleeve. The pain in his forearm is drilling, too deep and distinct, he suspects, for a mere bruise.

Patrice's cell phone is on his desk. Since Marina returned it to him on Friday, he has forgotten it more than once, clearly loath at some level to give #1 another chance to scare him. But he uses it to call a twenty-four-hour locksmith. Still recovering in the garage, George was hatcheted by a new fear. He had surrendered his house keys, and his address is on the driver's license in the wallet he handed over. When the khaki radioed the police, George asked, first thing, that they send a squad to watch his house.

He phones Patrice next to tell her the locksmith is on the way.

"I got carjacked and lost the keys."

"Oh my God, George. Are you all right?"

"I'm okay. It's my own fault. I've been warned a dozen times about hanging around in the parking garage. I saw those kids lurking, and I was trying to be a tough guy—" He stops, recognizing that he's about to reveal much of what he has been holding back. Instead, he asks Patrice to take a look out the front window. The black-andwhite is at the curb.

"But how are you?" she asks again when she's come back to the phone.

"Fine, fine. Shaken, naturally. I got a little frisky. I need to get an X-ray of my arm. Right now I'm waiting for the cops."

"An X-ray? I'm coming down there," she says.

The last thing she needs is more time at a hospital. And her return to work is certain to have worn her out. But the locksmith is reason enough that she shouldn't leave the house, and she finally accepts that.

"Between the police and the ER, I'll be hours," he says. He promises to wake her when he gets in.

Abel is peering in by the time he's off the phone.

"Jeez-o-Pete, Judge." He was paged at home and came running in green Bermuda shorts that reveal a pair of pink toothpick legs. It's a wonder of nature they can support his bulk.

"It's all on me, Abel. I should have listened to you."

Abel insists on seeing the judge's arm. For whatever reason, George has not actually looked, and he knows he's in trouble when the arm proves to be too swollen for him simply to roll up his sleeve. Instead, he has to unbutton his shirt. An alarming dome of sore-looking red-and-blue flesh has risen halfway between his wrist and elbow. Abel whistles at the sight.

"Judge, let's get you over to the hospital. The boys from Area Two can just as well take the report there."

In the ER at Masonic, George waits in a little curtained area for more than an hour before they get him to X-ray. The judge took the precaution of bringing some work, but his right arm hurts when he attempts to write, and his editing is confined to juvenile scratches in the margin whose meaning he hopes he will remember tomorrow.

"Hairline fracture," the ER doc says when he finally breezes in with the film. He gives George a blue canvas sling and Vicodin for the nights. Otherwise, the judge should be able to get by with an ibuprofen. "See an orthopedist in three days," the doc says when he sweeps back the curtain.

Out in the waiting room, Abel has inserted himself into one of the wooden armchairs. He's passing the time beside a man whom he introduces as a detective from Area 2. His name is Phil Cobberly, a heavy guy with tousled brown hair and a ruddy, alcoholic complexion. George shakes backhanded, using his left.

"You know, Judge, you and I did some business before," says Cobberly. "You had me on the stand in that *Domingo* case years ago. Remember? General Manager of one of these giant furniture outfits, jiggering the inventory and sending merchandise out the back door? Guy was making a bill and a half, and stealing anyway. I thought we had this character on the express to the slam. Six coppers on the surveillance?"

George recalls now. Cobberly testified at the preliminary hearing and, relying on the joint report the officers had filed, identified the position of every member of the major theft unit as they observed the crime. When George subpoenaed personnel records from McGrath Hall, it turned out that two of those officers had been on leave that night. It was sloppiness, not perjury, but with proof that the police had been willing to swear to more than they actually remembered, the P.A. pled the case for probation while the coppers seethed.

"'Course these little hair balls that done you," Cobberly says, "they won't have that kinda lawyer, right? Your clients paid the freight. These mutts'll stay put." Cobberly smiles and scratches his face. For him there's divine justice in seeing a guy who made good money freeing bad guys now on the receiving end of crime. George gave up trying to explain things to cops like this a long time ago.

Abel intervenes. "Judge is probably tired, Philly."

Having vented, Cobberly is amiable enough taking the report.

"What about the tats?" he asks eventually.

George says the only tattoo he saw was the five-pointed star of the Almighty Latin Nation on the boy's right hand.

"If he's courted in to Latinos Reyes," Cobberly says, speaking of the set that Corazón probably still heads, "then he should have had a crown right above that, same size."

"Maybe that's what he was looking for with this bit," Abel says, "kid that age. Blood for life," he adds. George thought the same thing himself when he believed he was going to get killed, but Abel's interpretation strikes him as a stretch given how things turned out. The gang initiations usually require violence—shooting, stabbing, stomping rivals—not stealing a Lexus.

"To me, it was a straight carjack, guys," George says. "Whatever I thought at first."

Neither Cobberly nor Abel are fully convinced, nor is Marina, who comes rushing in just as George and Abel are ready to depart. She too is in shorts, and a placket shirt, both designer items. Off the job, she looks quite stylish. She was on her way down-state for a morning conference when she received the page. By now, George is drained and sick of the hospital—the misery on wheels, the hubbub and brightness—but because Marina has driven 110 miles in two hours to get back, he's obliged to replay the whole incident, and they sit down together again in the waiting room outside the ER.

"I don't buy it as a coincidence, Judge. Look at the pattern. Corazón just keeps ramping it up one notch each time. Getting closer and closer. You say these kids have been watching you for close to a week, right? Like they were waiting for you?"

"I'd say they were waiting for anybody with a car key. I'm just the guy who got bingo, because I'm always stupid enough to sit around there. If Corazón meant to put me down, he'd never have had a clearer shot."

"He's got his own timetable, Judge. He sent those kids to do just what they did—jack you and scare all of us silly in the process."

George understands her theory. Corazón wants everybody—the cops, the prosecutors, and the judge most of all—to know the kill is coming. When it does, every soul who had a hand in putting Corazón away will reside in terror, seeing that the Inca of Los Latinos Reyes takes vengeance with impunity— and a smile, because the state itself will provide Corazón with a complete defense, given all its ironclad guarantees about the total isolation of prisoners in the supermax.

Call it denial, but George still thinks this is

police hype. Latinos Reyes are a street gang, not Mossad, and Corazón's hallmark is brutality, not calculating patience. But George isn't going to duke it out with Marina again.

When he stands to leave, she says, "It's 24/7 now, Judge. There'll be cops covering you whenever you leave the courthouse, and my people will have you there. No back talk."

He thinks it over. For the time being, this incident will serve as his explanation to Patrice.

His wife is sitting at the slate-topped kitchen island when George comes in, and he can tell something is wrong. She has dug out the bottle of Chivas they keep for guests, and there's a finger of brown liquid in her glass. Two decades ago, George decided that he needed to set some limits, and neither Patrice nor he usually drinks at home. But it's the merciless look she settles on him as he enters from the garage that's most telling.

"Death threats?" she asks then. "You've been getting death threats for weeks and never told me?"

The news has been on TV. 'A judge who has been receiving menacing e-mails for several weeks was attacked tonight in the courthouse parking garage but reportedly escaped with only minor injuries.' The phone has not stopped ringing—concerned friends and several reporters who somehow got the number and want a comment.

Caught out, George's first response is, "How did it get on TV?" But by now the cops know everything, and there is no such thing as a secret in McGrath Hall. Marina too might have spoken on background, knowing what the headline will be worth with the County Board.

"Do I really need to explain this?" he asks Patrice.

"Yes, you *really* need to explain this."

"I thought we were dealing with enough death threats in this house."

"Oh, George." She takes his good hand and blessedly lingers close, wraps herself around him. "No wonder you've been so loony." A marriage marches through so many stages of intimacy. The first, when you are convinced that the outer shells will melt away and make you one, is the most exalted, celebrated, and dramatic. But like a good lawyer, George can argue in behalf of others—the early moments of parenthood, when you try to figure out how to survive nature's slyest trick, using love to produce someone to come between you. Or this one. In sickness and in health.

"Is this why you were talking about not running?" she asks.

"Not really. Not for the most part."

"Well, what's 'the most part'? And please don't say me."

He tells her about Warnovits and Lolly Viccino. She listens to the whole story without letting go of his hand.

"You've been having a rough time, mate, haven't you?" She puts an arm around him again. "George," she says. "You are a good man. A very good man. It was another era. Things like that—It was vulgar, George. It was disgusting. But it wasn't criminal. Not then. Times change. Things get better. Humanity improves. And you get better with it. With the help of other human beings. That's what law's about. I don't have to give you that speech. You've been giving it to me for thirty years."

"And you haven't believed a word," he says, smiling.

She takes a second to consider.

"Well," she says, "at least I was listening."

They are still sitting together, talking about the effects of fear, what it takes from life and, oddly, adds, when he hears her cell phone buzz in the pocket of his jacket, which is hanging from his chair. He tells himself not to look, but Patrice stands to get the phone for him, and he reaches back rather than let her be the first to see the text message.

The screen says, "Next time 4 real. C U."

16
THE PUBLIC EYE

When George wakes up at 6:30 he can hear voices
outside, and he cracks one panel on the bedroom
shutters. Behind the black-and-white, which has
been positioned at the curb all night, three TV vans
have parked. Their long portable antennas, looking
like giant kitchen whisks, have been raised for
broadcast. Awaiting George's appearance, the crew
members from the competing stations are lounging
together against one of the vans, drinking their
coffee and shooting the breeze with the two cops
who are out there to guard the judge.

"Mate," he tells Patrice, "you aren't going to like this."

Marina arrives in a courthouse van an hour later. Three more cruisers have shown up as well. George calls Marina's cell to invite her into the house rather than appear outside and reward the camera crews for lying in wait.

"Shit," she says succinctly when he shows her the text message. "We gotta give this phone to the Bureau. See if they can set up some kind of trap. I can't believe he had the balls to do this again."

#1 clearly knows what Marina explained the other day about the difficulty of tracing text messages. And therefore did not care who had the cell phone now, law enforcement or George. He'd get the message either way.

"Maybe you should think about staying here, Judge."

"Good luck talking sense to him," Patrice says.

But George knows he's being prudent. Today every local security resource will be dedicated to his protection. He'll be safer than the President. And it would send the wrong message to stay home and cower. He took this job recognizing that the responsibilities are often symbolic.

Patrice continues peeking through the curtains to inspect the growing crowd on the parkway. There are at least a dozen journalists now, as well as eight cops and, naturally, quite a few of their neighbors. Patrice is having fits about the fate of everything she labored to plant this spring, an act of love and dedication that required energy she didn't really have so soon after surgery.

At 8:30, George opens his front door, feeling for all the world like he is entering a stage set. His arm remains too sore for any thought of abandoning the sling, and so his coat is draped across his right shoulder in the fashion of somebody who got winged in a western. Eyes forward, he endeavors to appear pleasant but businesslike and speaks not a word as the camerafolk and reporters dash beside him along his front walk.

Looking more officious than a general, Marina marches a step ahead of him while Abel alights to sweep open the van door. On George's behalf, Marina recites a one-line statement George and she composed inside—'The judge is feeling well and looks forward to conducting the business of the court'—while the cameramen jostle one another for the chance to poke their huge black lenses through the open window on the driver's side of the van. Screwing up his courage, George glances back to the line of little white sweet alyssum that have been trampled along the edging of the walk.

The vehicles take off in a convoy, one cruiser in front of Marina's van and another behind, while the TV trucks zoom up and drop back for camera angles. He considers how this is going to play on the news and laughs.

"What?" Marina asks.

"Private joke." After this star turn as urban war hero, George realizes he could not only free the *Warnovits* defendants but order the state to pay them reparations and still win the retention election.

The morning is a procession of visitors to chambers expressing sympathy, as well as constant phone calls from friends and reporters, which George does not take. The only persons he can't defer are his colleagues on the court. The Chief, appropriately, is the first to show up, instants after George has reached his chambers. He requires a full rundown of last night's events, shaking his head throughout.

"Nathan is bonkers," he says then. "He's sure he's next. I'll bet he's found himself a 'secure location' that's not within three hundred miles."

Neither of them can keep from laughing.

"So what's your theory?" Rusty asks. "About last night?"

Unrelated events, George explains, except that attempting to be bold in the face #1's threats seems to have made him more stupid.

"Still not buying Corazón?"

Strangely, only now, after avoiding it for weeks, the fear that properly belongs with that possibility invades the judge. His heart knocks and his hands clench as he imagines what it would mean to be stalked with lethal intent by a ruthless sociopath like Corazón. With his self-imposed exile, Koll might have the right approach if that actually were what is happening. But in his heart of hearts, George still does not believe it.

"To me, it doesn't fit," he tells the Chief. "But

the only way we'll ever know for sure is if the cops scoop up those kids and see whether they have any connection to Latinos Reyes. And I wouldn't bet a lot on that happening. My car's probably been peddled or chopped and those kids are high on the money."

"Probably," Rusty agrees.

By noon, the last of his visitors seem to have paid their respects. George is closing his door in hopes of getting some work done, but hearing it scrape over the carpet, Dineesha abruptly stands. Her hands folded across her plump middle, she faces him with an expectant look. She is handsome, if matronly, with a large globe hairdo, a seventies remnant she never abandoned. He motions her in with a leaden heart. He has seen her hangdog expression a thousand times before and knows just what's coming. There is only one cause.

"Zeke says the police talked to him, Judge, wanting to know where he was Friday. And he was in St. Louis, Judge. I'm sure. We had his dog while he was gone. And he says he had papers showing he went."

"I don't think anyone doubts that, Dineesha."

"The thing is, Judge, this is a good job for him. But if the police call the company, Judge. Well—" Her hands are still clasped in front of her waist. There's no point in asking whether Zeke truthfully answered the question on the employment application about whether he'd ever been convicted of a felony. For a guy like Zeke, it's all a circle anyway. Do it the right way and you'll never get your foot through the door.

"I don't think that's going to happen," he tells her. She sighs and smiles. "But one thing that bothered the police is that they thought you told Zeke to expect them."

Her mouth forms a dark O.

"It wasn't like that, Judge. I just had it out with him, Thursday night. I wasn't trying to warn him, just give him a piece of my mind. Judge, he says he wouldn't ever do you any harm. I believe it, Judge."

That's the problem, of course. His mother will always believe Zeke. No other sane person should.

"Dineesha, you don't really believe he and his pal were up here to use the bathroom, do you?"

She wilts with the question and takes a seat in the same straight-backed chair by the door that she found the other day in order to weep out of sight about her oldest child.

"No, Judge. I don't think that."

"So what were they doing? Were they here to steal something?"

She manages a quick, sharp laugh. "No, Judge. Just the opposite. They were putting something back."

"From my chambers?"

"From my purse. Zeke had been by that morning, Judge. Because of the dog. And he'd grabbed hold of my keys out of my purse."

"And why was that?"

She presses her finger to the center of her lips, determined not to cry again.

"He wanted to get into our shed. We stored his things when he went off, Judge." Prison is what she means. "And I don't know how exactly, but Reggie found two guns in there, and when Zeke came out, his father wouldn't let him have them. You know, he can't own firearms."

It's both a federal and a state crime for a felon even to hold a gun.

"And Reggie and Zeke, they go around about

those guns every couple of months. Zeke says all he wants is just to sell them, that they're worth good money. So he took my keys and got them. That boy Khaleel, he has the guns now, but I guess they made a deal, Khaleel was supposed to walk in and put the keys on my desk when I got up for a second, and if anybody saw that, he'd just say he'd found them in the hall, right outside the door."

She has her face in both hands.

"Judge, if he could just get himself going in the right direction, he'd really be all right. I truly believe that."

There is no divorcing your children, George thinks. For Dineesha, hope is eternal. And thus, so is the heartbreak.

"I mean, Judge, I don't have any right—"

"I'll keep it to myself, Dineesha." She stands, still under the weight of it.

Ten minutes later she knocks again. No more, George thinks. Even for Dineesha. But when she opens the door, he can see she has regathered herself. This is business.

"Murph's on the phone, Judge," she says. "Area Two picked up two boys. They want you for a lineup."

17
AREA 2

Area 2 headquarters is a fortress, a limestone redoubt
built near the turn of the century. It is frequently
shot by TV and movie crews when they need an
exterior that appears utterly impregnable. Entering,
you confront a much newer cinder-block wall,
interrupted only by a small window of bulletproof
glass, behind which the desk officer sits. Years ago
there was a little metal teller's tray at the bottom
so bondsmen or relatives could pass bail money,
but that was before some gangster stuck a sawed-off
in the slot and seriously wounded three officers.

These days everybody passes first through a metal detector.

Cobberly, the red-faced detective who enjoyed giving it to George last night, is on the other side.

"So what do we know about these fine young lads, Philly?" Abel asks him. On the way over, Abel said that the younger boy had been grabbed in a nod in George's Lexus, which was parked on a North End street. An hour later, the older one strolled up with the car key and a sack of burgers.

According to Phil Cobberly, the two are brothers, the last of four.

"Nice family," the detective says. "Dad was always in and out of the joint, but now there's sort of a family reunion. Older two boys are in Rudyard with him. I just love happy endings," he adds.

"Bangers?" George asks.

"Natch."

"Latinos Reyes?"

"Nope. Over where they're from in Kewahnee, that's Two-Six turf." Twenty-sixth Street Locos.

"So no connection to Corazón?"

"Can't say that. Two-Six and Latinos Reyes make their deals."

Abel asks if the boys gave any statements.

"Usual speeches," says Cobberly, "don't know nothin', but we didn't take it down. They're juvie."

Juveniles may not be questioned outside the presence of their parents, who, in Area 2, do not tend to answer when the police come knocking. In their absence, a youth officer must attend the interview. The State Defender assigned to the station was summoned too, since both boys will be charged as adults. He, in turn, called for his supervisor. George suspects he is the reason a higher-up was needed. The State Defenders want to tread carefully with a judge, especially one on the appellate court who sides with them occasionally.

When the supervisor arrives, it turns out to be Gina Devore, who oversaw the S.D.s in George's courtroom during the two years he sat at the trial level in the Central Branch. She was famous in the courthouse for punching out one of her clients in the lockup when he grabbed her breast. Five feet in her heels, Gina knocked the guy cold.

"The best and brightest," George greets her. She surprises him a bit with a quick hug despite being on duty. Married to a police lieutenant in Nearing, she gives him a one-sentence rundown on both of her kids.

"How's the arm, Judge? I heard about you on TV."

"It's all right, but I don't think I'll be sending your clients a thank-you note."

"Judge," she says, "I bet when you get a look, you'll realize they've got the wrong kids." She is utterly stone-faced making that remark, although both George and she know that not only were these boys arrested in the judge's car, but each kid's clothing—and the guns discovered under the front seats—matched his descriptions.

The boys' defense, if it goes according to the book, will be that they found the Lexus abandoned with the key in the ignition. It's farfetched at best. But if George makes the IDs, the case becomes a lock. No jury will disbelieve a judge in these circumstances.

Led by the Detective Commander, Len Grissom, a bony, self-contained Texan, the procession—two defense lawyers, a Deputy P.A. named Adams who has arrived from Felony Review, Cobberly, Abel, and several other officers, and, finally, the judge—enters the shift room, where the Area 2 cops assemble to start duty. It looks like a classroom, full of school chairs with plastic desk extensions on the right arms. In front, a track of high-wattage flood-lights blares down. They were installed for lineups, both to illuminate the participants and to prevent them from getting a good look at the witnesses.

Four boys parade out and spread themselves along the platform from which, at other times, the shift sergeant makes the day's assignments. They are all between five six and five nine, the height George gave for his second assailant. Three of the kids are probably volunteers from the juvie house who will be rewarded for their cooperation with a hamburger in the squad car on the way back. They all wear blue jail coveralls, but a sweatshirt is passed from one to the next. Each puts it on for a second and draws the hood around his face, then turns to expose both profiles.

By the time the fashion show, as it's called, has ended, George has settled on the third boy from the left. Gina clearly does not like the array and scrib-bles notes on her yellow pad. The problem is obvious. Two of the kids don't have the close-cropped hair George described on the younger boy, but even with that hint, he is not quite positive about the kid he's inclined to identify. From the corner of his eye, the judge catches Cobberly scratching his face. He uses three fingers and rakes his nails across his cheek three times, repeating this performance twice more. George says nothing but stares until Gina's younger colleague catches on.

"What?" Cobberly says.

"Can we get that dipstick out of here?" Gina asks Grissom. She looks at George. "Did you know him?"

"Sixty, seventy percent," he tells her. "I'd have said, 'Most closely resembles.'" The lawyers make notes.

It takes more than half an hour for the second array of taller boys to appear because Gina has demanded that Grissom find sweatshirts for all of them, and each emerges with the hood drawn around his face, depriving George of any clues from their hair.

He asks Gina, "Do you mind if I get closer?"

George walks along only a few feet from the platform. Gina has asked Grissom to instruct all the participants to look only straight ahead, but when George strolls by, the fourth in the group, the kid he's ready to make, can't resist a peek downward. His eyes do not rest long, but he might as well have shaken hands and called George '*puto*' for old times' sake.

The judge stops there and points.

"Oh, man," the kid says, but it's fairly faint-hearted. After Cobberly's stunt, the other cops are careful not even to glance in George's direction, but he knows from a pulse in the room that he selected the right boy.

Next, Grissom leads George and the legal retinue behind him to the desk of one of the detectives. Six handguns are laid out, two of them undoubtedly recovered from the boys under arrest. George knew nothing about firearms when he started as a State Defender, but he learned more than he might have liked on the job, and he has remained somewhat up-to-date because he often reads trial transcripts of the testimony of ballistics experts. He thought the silver gun with black handles that the older boy held on him was a Kahr MK40, which he recognized only because it's the current king of concealed weapons. It was probably 'rented' from a senior gang member in exchange for a share of the proceeds. The second kid had a black .32 or .38, also an automatic. George picks out the first gun without hesitating. The courtroom axiom is true. It's the only thing you really see. He takes a guess at the second.

"So much for the unreliability of eyewitness testimony," Gina murmurs. With the IDs made, George and Abel and Gina await the cops who have remained behind in the detectives' area with the Deputy P.A. from Felony Review, caucusing to be certain that they need nothing more to make their case.

"Neither gun was loaded by the way," Gina says to George, as they're waiting. "Just for the record."

"Pros, huh?" Abel asks.

"Not first-timers. But it counts, right? Not to take a chance on killing somebody?"

"Except by heart attack," the judge says.

The cops and P.A.s are bound to be satisfied, but from George's perspective, picking out the right kids is only a start. The real issue is whether Corazón sent them. Gina will never let the boys talk to the cops, especially if Cobberly or anybody like him is involved. George keeps turning the problem over.

"How would you react if I said I wanted to interview your client?" the judge asks her. "The taller one?"

"What's he get?" Gina responds instantly.

"I'm not in charge."

She smiles. "Something tells me everybody will listen pretty hard to the recommendations of an appellate court judge."

"So then, let's see if he spills. It's the one way he can lighten the load on this thing."

When the cops emerge, Grissom likes the idea. "You'll get more from this kid than we will, Judge," he says.

Gina goes off to inform her client.

The boy is placed in a beaten-up interrogation room with an old wooden desk and three chairs and a number of heel scuffs and gouges running up the walls. From the corridor, he can be viewed through a one-way mirror. Nonetheless Grissom, Gina, and the P.A. escort George into the room and remain standing behind him while the judge takes a chair opposite the kid. There's an iron hook in the floor used to chain the prisoners who are shackled, but as a juvenile, the boy is merely cuffed. By the terms Gina established, her client will not get renewed Miranda warnings, meaning his statements can't be used against him in court, on the odd chance he ends up going to trial.

"Man, you got me down bad, man," he tells George. He's talking about the lineup.

"How's that?"

"Man, I ain' never seen you before. Never, man."

"It didn't look to me like your eyes were closed last night, so I don't think I believe that."

"Nuh-uh, man. You got me down bad." The kid has a round face, a hawk's nose, and large, dark eyes, quick with concern. The half-head of raven hair shines on the back of his scalp. Even lying, he looks a good deal more appealing than he did when he was holding a gun.

Gina speaks up behind George.

"Hector," she says, "didn't you listen? I told you, you have two choices. Either shut up or tell the judge you're sorry and answer his questions straight down. Nobody wants to hear that you weren't there last night."

"*Es verdad*, man," Hector says.

"Cut it out," Gina says. "Listen to what the judge wants to know, and do yourself some good."

Hector responds to the word *judge* this time.

"You a judge?" When George nods, the brief lick of a smile crosses Hector's lips. He jacked a judge. There will be some street cred for that. But the smile slips away as the young man reflects further. In his face, you can see the digits falling and his mounting concern. "So how's this go, man? You ain't gonna be the judge on me, man, right?"

"Nope."

"Just gonna be one of your people, right?"

"Not necessarily."

"Yeah," Hector says. He doesn't believe it for a second. His tongue slides around in his mouth as he assesses his predicament. Then his black eyes kick up to George with an aspect of surprising openness.

"So how's that anyway, man?" he asks.

"What?"

"You know, man, sittin' up there, goin' like, 'You guilty, man. You ain' guilty. Dude, you get twenty-five. But you, *hombre*, you get paper.'" Hector's cuffed hands circle the air as he passes out these imaginary sentences. "That cool or what?"

"That's not actually my job anymore," George says. "But when I did it, I never especially enjoyed that part." George has never met a judge who didn't say that sentencing is the hardest thing he or she has to do.

"*Ese,*" the kid answers, "is pretty cool." When George was a State Defender and had conversations like this, he used to give his young clients the same timeworn speech. Forget thug life, stay in school, you can be a lawyer too. It was 1973, and George believed that. He hears occasionally from a couple of the young men he represented who turned their lives around, but nobody's a lawyer or a judge. These days kids like Hector sneer. At the age of sixteen, he already knows how much of the world is closed to him.

"Hector, I want to know why you and your brother decided to rob me."

"Man, I don't know nothin' 'bout who jacked you, man. But gotta be to see the presidents, no?" Money, he means.

"Maybe we should ask Guillermo," Grissom says from behind, referring to the little brother.

"Oh, he's soft, man. You can't go with nothin' he gonna tell you. He's just off the hook, man."

Nonetheless, Grissom's made his point. Hector seems to sober.

"That arm broke, man?" He nods at George's sling.

"Hairline fracture. Hurts."

"Y *que*," says Hector again. "Gotta do your work, right?"

"If that's what you call it." George gives the boy a cold look. "I want to know why you jacked me, Hector. I want the whole story. It's the only way Guillermo and you catch a break."

Hector ponders while George keeps a hard eye on him.

"Y *que*," the kid says wearily again and takes a deep breath in defeat. "We got this *carnal*, man. Fortuna? Had his first appearance and all last week. And that judge, man, he did him real greasy. Twenty bills, man. The bond? And he's just hemmed in on some little dope thing, man. Twenty bills? What's up with that, man? So like, Billy and me, man—you know, we was gonna back him up."

"Help him make bond?"

Hector nods. "We seen you, man? Just sittin' there? Couple times we seen you. So, you know, we get us the *cuetes*. But Billy, man, we come up on you, and he's like, 'No, *vato*, no way we can do this *hombre*, man, he's like prayin'.' Were you prayin' in that car?"

George can't help smiling briefly.

"But why me, Hector, and not somebody else?"

The boy draws back with a quick, disdaining look.

"Man, that's a nice g-ride, man, ain't that? *Mucho ferria*." A lot of change.

George would have been skeptical that a 1994 Lexus, a virtual antique, commands much on the street, but Cobberly said the Mexican gangs prefer to detail and retrofit older cars, regarded as classics. A style born of need is now fashion.

"Nobody pointed me out? Described the car?"

"Man, you was there. We was there. No way I knew you was a judge, man. Nothin' like that. Only thing I heard is after, when we went to that lame puke who said he was gonna take it off us, and he's goin' like, '*Malo suerte*, man, that ride, it's been on TV, I ain' gonna touch it.' Even he didn't say 'Judge,' man." Hector shakes his head over his ill fortune.

"What about the guy you got the guns from?" George asks. "You didn't talk about it with him?"

"Jorge? Can't tell him nothin', man. He'd come over and do you himself." The kid frowns. "Jorge, man, that's gonna be one *vato loco* 'bout losin' them weapons."

"How about this, Hector? Do you know the name Jaime Colon? El Corazón?"

George has asked the question in his best matter-of-fact tone, but it stops Hector cold. He rears back and delivers a narrow, disbelieving look.

"Corazón?"

"You know who he is?"

"*Ese.* You thin' I don't know Corazón? Seen him plenty, man."

The judge takes care to show nothing.

"Where have you seen him?"

Hector looks to the distance to fix the time.

"Tuesday night, man, ain't it? My ma, man, she don't never miss them damn *telenovelas*. She *loves* that guy, man. '*Mira, mira, El Corazón.*' She's straight *loca* about him."

On the way out of the room, Gina grabs George.

"Did you believe him?"

"More or less."

"I want three for him. And two for the little brother. The guns weren't loaded."

"That's too light."

"Come on, Judge. First adult offense."

He remembers how he felt facing that pistol. His instinct is to say six, but that's what the *Warnovits* defendants got for raping Mindy DeBoyer.

"Gina, my arm's in a sling. And both those boys have chairs with their names on them in juvie court. Five and three sounds right to me. That's what I'll tell the P.A."

Marina, who came speeding back from her conference after the arrests, missed the interrogation. She's just entering from the receiving area as George and Abel are headed to the door. Grissom comes over, and together the three of them describe what's transpired. Marina asks several questions before they leave.

"What do you think?" George asks her as they depart the station. She appears somewhat listless, without her usual brio. Then again, given events in the garage and her travel schedule, she missed a night's sleep.

"I don't think anybody in his right mind gives up Corazón—six, sixteen, or sixty."

George tries not to react, but compared with Marina, Ahab barely gave a second thought to that fish.

"Not that it matters anymore," she adds.

"Why doesn't it matter?"

"I got a call from the FBI, Judge, while we were driving back. Remember I told you they were going to run forensic software on your hard drive? When I shipped Koll's letter over, it sort of reminded them. They only picked up one thing, but it's pretty interesting. The very first e-mail you got, Judge? They figured out what computer it came from."

"And?"

Weary, Marina nonetheless manages to find his eye.

"It was yours. The one in your chambers."

18

COMPUTER RESEARCH

George stands on the sidewalk outside Area 2 with Marina and Abel, trying to gather himself. It's shift change, and the black-and-whites are double-parked in the small lot behind the station while uniformed officers, usually in pairs, stroll in and out in the declining light of a mild late-spring evening. Across the street, in a ragged park, a few flowering trees remain in bloom on a lawn that is littered and unmowed. George's arm is bothering him. He needs more ibuprofen.

"My computer?" he asks. "The first message came from my computer?"

"Yes, sir," Marina answers. "They finally got around to running the forensic software and reconstructing your hard drive, so they could see everything that had been on it. I mean, it's an obvious thought that a message returned to your computer came from there. But since the rest of the e-mails went through the open relay, the Bureau techies pretty much crossed that off. They only ran the forensic software to double-check on your copy of the message Koll received, to see if there was something about it they hadn't noticed, but as long as they were doing it, the techs poked around to look at the very first e-mail—the one you thought you'd deleted?—and when they reconstructed the message, it was like, 'Whoa!' It was from your IP address, through the courthouse server. That seemed pretty weird because there was no copy in your Sent file. They figured it was a super-sophisticated spoof, and then one of them suggested reconstructing the Sent file too, and there it was. It'd been deleted."

"And what about the other e-mails I got?"

"Nope. The Bureau says the first is the only one

sent from your machine. The rest just mimicked your address—there's no sign of them on your hard drive."

"So what's the thinking, Marina? I've been threatening myself?"

Marina's mouth rolls around. "Are you asking me or are you asking the Bureau?" she answers finally.

"Oh, for Chrissake" is all George can say.

"I mean, Judge. It wouldn't be the first time some attention-seeking meatball threatened himself. It happens all the time."

That's why the Bureau ran the forensic software. Because it dawned on someone that they hadn't crossed the first logical suspect off the list. Even in his irritation, George realizes that, as a perpetrator, he probably makes more sense than Corazón.

"Marina, I was sitting there with John Banion when one of those early messages arrived. The one where we called you? I couldn't have sent it to myself."

She hitches a shoulder. "It can be twenty minutes, Judge, from sending to receipt."

"And what's my motive?" But that's clear, when

he reflects for an instant. He's running for retention, after all, and can benefit from appearing a hero to the public. "Do they figure I arranged to get my arm broken too?"

"It's a theory, Judge. You think I'd be talking to you like this if I believed it?"

Ten count, he thinks, and recites each number to himself slowly.

"But let's figure out who it *is*," she says, "and leave present company aside. We're looking for somebody who had access to your computer."

"No one has access to my computer. Seriously, Marina. Anybody who sat down in my chair and started typing would have a lot of questions to answer."

"It wouldn't take thirty seconds to type out 'You'll pay,' when you'd stepped out."

Trying to unscramble all of this, George thinks back to the initial messages.

"So if I understand," he says, "the first e-mail, the one that says 'You'll pay,' comes from my computer. And then someone sends me the identical message twice the same day from another computer?"

"Right."

"Why?"

"Obviously, to get your attention."

"No. I mean why use my computer in the first place? Were we supposed to have noticed this a long time ago? Is it like the messages to my cell phone? Or my home? Number One showing how easily he can invade my space?"

An eyebrow flares. "What messages to your home?"

"Just one," George says, but for a second he's afraid she's going to slap him.

"You are a lousy, lousy patient," Marina says finally.

"Duly noted."

She takes another instant to calm down. Now they are more or less even, both aggravated and trying to put it aside.

"Well," she says finally, "if you were supposed to notice that the e-mail came from your computer, Judge, why would somebody delete it? The techs say both copies—the received message and the retained copy of what was sent—were removed simultaneously. About six hours after it initially went out."

"Meaning it wasn't deleted by accident?"

"Doesn't look like it."

"I'm lost," George says.

"Okay," Marina says, "but let's work this through. We're talking about somebody who could walk into your chambers when you weren't there and not be noticed. Twice that day. You tell me who that is."

"Do they know the timing on all of this?"

Marina's little notebook is in the pocket of her khaki sport coat.

"Sent 9:42 A.M. And then it gets deleted from both files a little before four."

"So there are definitely other people around chambers both times?"

"Seems likely. Does anybody besides you know the password on your computer?"

"Dineesha."

"Just Dineesha?"

The truth lands on him like something from the sky. Zeke. Zeke after all. It's a proven fact that he freely rifles his mother's things. She has the password written somewhere, and Zeke found it. The judge speaks his name.

"Great minds," says Marina. "That was what hit

me when I heard from the Bureau. But that first message, that was sent on a Friday. When Zeke was supposed to be down in St. Louis. And we just called the company to confirm he was there. He's clear."

Clear, but also unemployed, George thinks. Zeke's employer in St. Louis won't keep him a day after receiving questions from the FBI. So it goes for Zeke. This is the other side of his story. But, as always, it's Zeke's mother George feels for the most.

"All right," he says. "Where were we?"

"Password on your computer? Only Dineesha has it."

"Right." He thinks. "But if I'd been using the computer and went down the hall for a minute, the security screen wouldn't cycle back on for what, fifteen minutes?"

"Should be ten," Marina says. "So let's say it's somebody who walked in at that point and typed for just a second. Who could that be?"

"Anybody on my staff."

"Okay. That's got to be our priority group. Because of the timing. Who else could just go cruising in there?"

"Sometimes another judge comes by to drop off a draft. These days we usually e-mail, but now and then there's an issue to talk over, and one of my brethren will hand-carry his or her opinion to me. I suppose if I was out the first time, she or he would have an excuse to come back."

"And can we figure out which judges you were working with?"

"It's end of term, Marina. In the last month, I've probably exchanged drafts with every member of the court from the Chief on down."

"Okay. So we rule in your staff. The judges. And?"

"Maybe their clerks. It's possible. But if we're talking about somebody who could just walk past Dineesha, then we'd have to include people from your shop. Murph and you."

"We'll put me on the suspect list right behind you. Who else?"

"IS. Maintenance. That's about it."

"Okay. So where do we start?"

"Start what?"

"Well, I'd like to question your staff."

George knows what that will be like. Bare-knuckles

interrogation. Dineesha, John, Cassie, Marcus. They'll be hot-boxed, accused. He doesn't like the idea at all and says so.

"Do you have a best guess, Judge? Somebody who should be first?"

"Can I think about it overnight?"

Marina agrees. Abel will drive George back to the courthouse, then home. They have reached the van when George snaps his fingers and trots back into the station to see Grissom.

"I forgot," he says. "Where's my car?"

It's at the pound, in the hands of the evidence techs. Even expediting everything—lifts, vacuuming, photographs—it will be a few days before the P.A.'s office signs off on the release.

Grissom gives him a little smile. "Besides, you're not thinking of driving now, Judge, are you? Not before you get that arm out of a sling."

"Law enforcement," George says to Abel when he climbs into the van.

In chambers, he finds that Banion, ever faithful, has left papers on his chair, printouts from a periodical database. It's a moment before George fathoms the point. It's a listing of articles by authors named Lolly or Viccino. On the bottom of page one, there are four entries from quilting journals by somebody named Lolly Viccino Gardner. John has used another search engine to find a phone and an address in Livermore, California, which he's written in the margin in his tidy hand.

George checks his watch. Two hours earlier there.

"I'll be a few minutes, Abel," he calls. Lounged on the green sofa and engrossed in a paperback novel about cops, Abel merely waves as George closes the door.

Why? he asks himself. But he's already dialing. It rings four times, and whoever says hello sounds a bit breathless, as if she ran.

"My name is George Mason. Judge George Mason. I'm hoping to speak to a woman named Lolly Viccino—or who used to go by that name."

Time passes. "Speaking."

"And are you the Lolly Viccino who attended Columa College in 1964?" he asks, although he knows he's found her from the little wrinkle of a Tidewater accent in the lone word she's uttered.

Lolly Viccino, in the meantime, is engaged in calculations of her own.

"Is this about money? Are you raising money for that place? Because, brother, you're barking up the wrong tree."

"No, ma'am," he answers, realizing that he himself sounds a little as he might have forty years ago. "Hardly that. No."

"And you say you're a judge?"

He repeats his title. "In DuSable."

"DuSable. I've never been there. Are you sure you've got the right person?"

"No, no," he says. "This isn't official business."

"Oh," she says. "I hoped you were calling to tell me I'd inherited a fortune from a long-lost relative." She laughs then, a little trick of sound raveled by bitterness.

"Afraid not," he says.

"Well, why then?"

He finally says he'd been an undergrad at Charlottesville.

"And did I know you?" she asks.

"I think so."

"Did we go out? I'm not sure I dated anybody there."

"No," he agrees.

"How was it we met?"

So here he is. There's no way he can get the words out of his mouth. And it would be cruel to remind her of something she's stored away, whether conveniently or with some measure of pain. Even the day after the event, he wasn't sure how much she'd retained. He never answers.

"Because I don't think about any of that," she adds then. "I never go back to that part of the world. Do you?"

He doesn't actually. Not since his parents died. Both his sisters are in Connecticut. He has surrendered his Virginia citizenship, as it were. And so has Lolly Viccino.

"It's all so old there," she says. "I'm just happy to be gone. I don't talk to any of them from home, to tell you the truth. And how did you say I know you?"

"I just have a memory," he says, "of bumping into you. During Party Weekend in the fall. And

264

I've been thinking about some things that happened back then."

"Well, I'm sure I wouldn't remember. I can't even picture anything from that time. I hated all of it."

"Oh," he says.

"So I'm afraid I can't help you, Judge. Mason?"

"Yes."

She lingers then. Of course, she thinks she knows the name. Which she does. You can't grow up in Virginia without hearing of George Mason. They named a university for him, and roads. Saving that, George is certain she would have hung up moments ago.

"I suppose," he says, "I suppose I've been curious about how your life turned out."

"Really? And why is that? How did *your* life turn out?"

"Pretty well," he responds instantly. "Very well." That, in fact, has been the unvoiced question of the last few months, and this, he realizes, is his answer. He has most of what he ever wanted. He's been able to say that for quite some time, especially since he reached the Court of Appeals. His family's always been A minus to A plus, depending on the moment. Judge Mason gets up most mornings knowing that life worked out better for him than for most people.

"I can't say that," she says. "I get by. I've gotten by. But I'm here, you know? One day at a time. That's how it is for everybody, right? It's not easy for anybody, Judge, is it?"

"Well, I'm sorry for anything I did to make it harder," he replies. If you had pressed him for an answer when he lifted the phone, he would have said that he was calling her to help decide a case. He thought he might have been searching for Lolly to see how much damage had been done, and how angry she remained four decades later. Or to try to confirm his current interpretations. Did she think she had been trying to punish or debase herself when she hooked up with Hugh Brierly and his roommate, or had she simply suffered from one of those boundless, youthful misapprehensions of what might be fun? Had she been deceived somehow? Or even coerced? Or was it possible, if he were being unsparing, that the incident did not stand alone? But it turns out that his greatest desire is to address her as someone who has profited from his life and now knows better. Who looks back with regret. Who wishes he made something sweet, rather than cruel, out of what was inevitably a momentous instant in his life, for his sake, first, and also for hers. And to tell her that.

"Oh, brother," Lolly Viccino says in response. "Get in line. Are you in AA?"

"No."

"Because those people always want you to get hold of somebody you haven't seen since Noah and tell them you're sorry. That's why I quit," she says. "I didn't see the sense of that. Who forgives me for all the stupid crap I did? Nobody. That's for sure. Just go on. That's what you have to do. You can't change the past, right, Judge? Am I right? So forget it. That's my attitude."

"I see," he says.

"That's how some people are. That's how I am. So I'm afraid I can't help you. Whatever it is, it's all ancient history."

"Of course."

"So thank you for calling, Judge." Now that she has reaffirmed the motto she lives by, she seems determined to get away before he can remind her of anything else. Then someone speaks behind her, a woman whose arrival only seems to hasten Lolly's desire to end the conversation. The last word he hears from her as the phone is going down is "Strange."

19

CASSIE

George Mason has known Cassandra Oakey all her life. He held her no more than a month after she was born, and he retains a clear memory of playing Go Fish with her for an entire afternoon when she was seven and had come to the office with Harrison on a school holiday while George was in the life-suspended state that always set in when he was waiting for a jury. Harry, ever the cheerleader, dragged George to several of Cassie's high school tennis matches, when she played number two on a conference championship team. She lacked quickness, but she was a determined and powerful player, with a serve like a mortar.

But Cassie Oakey can—and does—walk in and out of the judge's chambers with impunity, and among his staff, she would approach George's personal computer with the least natural trepidation. Far more telling, Cassie Oakey was the only staff member with him at the Hotel Gresham when his cell phone disappeared. And Cassie is leaving in two weeks, apparently with a sense of unrelieved injury.

"It has to be somebody who works in chambers," George explains to Patrice as they eat dinner in the kitchen, picking over the leftovers of a restaurant meal from two plastic containers. "It's not realistic that anyone else would be able to steal on to my computer twice in the same day when I wasn't around. Cassie's office is right there. Who else could get in and out so quickly?"

"I don't believe it," says Patrice.

"I don't believe it of any of them. Dineesha?"

"That's ridiculous."

"Banion's been with me nearly nine years. Marcus—I mean people can surprise you, but if Marcus is a computer whiz—"

"No," Patrice says definitively about George's hoary bailiff.

"No." He had reached the same conclusion about Cassie while he was speaking to Marina at Area 2 but wanted time to disprove it to himself. Her motive remains elusive. Harrison is often a practical joker, and George wonders if perhaps this started as some kind of prank, which she could not acknowledge when it turned out that no one saw the humor. "It's got to be some psychiatric mish-mash. Don't you think? Some issue with her father? It just makes no sense."

Patrice groans then. "What will you say to Harry and Miranda?"

In response, he emits a similar sound. But the judge will have to confront his clerk, if for no other reason than to save her from herself. The threat to Nathan Koll means that George cannot quietly excuse this escapade on his own. Besides, Marina is going to review her notes tonight and realize that only Cassie was with him at the luncheon. His clerk will have to resign tomorrow to avoid Marina's inquisition and to gain control of events that could ultimately imperil her law license. Always the defense lawyer, George is already thinking how he can smooth this over if Cassie fesses up quickly. He'll need Rusty's help, which is not guaranteed. We all run true to form, and Rusty, after all, started as a prosecutor.

George calls Cassie at home a little after 8:30 P.M. Something urgent, he says. Can she meet him for breakfast at 8:00?

Predictably, she more or less insists on knowing what this is about. "Is it *Warnovits*? Have you finally made up your mind?"

"Well, that's one thing," he says. Since his conversation with Lolly this afternoon, the case, for the first time in weeks, seems less like his own dose of iodine-131, beaming destructive rays through his body. "I've decided I want to write a draft myself. A matter like this probably justifies being a little more expansive." George's opinions normally run lean. His ingrained view of judging is to decide only what needs to be resolved and with as few words as possible.

"What did I mess up?" she asks at once. "Is it the limitations stuff?"

"Your work was as good as always. I'm sure I'll use a lot of it, and ask for your help. I just want to lay my own hand on this to start." It occurs to him that this is a pointless discussion. Cassie is going to be gone from chambers by tomorrow afternoon.

"So what else do you want to talk about?"

"It will be better in person."

She sighs with her characteristic absence of deference, indicating that George is being a pain.

"Where?"

He gave that question some thought before picking up the phone and had an inspiration.

"How about the Hotel Gresham?" If Cassie has a conscience, and he remains confident she does, she'll be uneasy there, perhaps quicker to admit what she's done. Predictably, she objects that the hotel is too far from chambers.

"The only place in town I eat bacon," George says. "Hand-cut and Virginia-cured. When you sin, Cassandra, you always go back to your roots."

*

George does not think about his security convoy until he wakes. Police protection is unneeded now, since there's no evidence that Cassie is engaged in anything other than psychological warfare. Nevertheless, somebody will probably show up. Marina figures to be slow to admit things were not as she suspected. And then again, there's the practical problem that George needs a ride to work. He leaves a voice message for Marina saying that he'll make his own way to the courthouse and calls a taxi, arriving at the Hotel Gresham by half past seven. He stands in the gaudy lobby, a remnant of the Gilded Age, with marble columns the size of sequoias and a ceiling encrusted with gilt and cherubim, while he tries to recall the whereabouts of the Salon, where breakfast is served.

A plump, amiable security guard in a blazer, with a white earpiece peeking under her hairdo, approaches to offer help.

"You're the judge, right? I saw you on TV the other night. How you doin'?"

In the last twenty-four hours, he has frequently found himself the object of staring, a distinctly uncomfortable experience. His father always disapproved of calling attention to oneself.

"I think the arm's a lot better this morning."

"Glad to hear that. We all were talking about you yesterday. I was sure when I heard that on the news, I knew you. You're the judge who lost his cell phone here last month, right?"

When he nods, she lights up, pleased by the potency of her memory.

"You got it back now, don't you?"

"Nope. It never showed up."

"Now how can that be? I thought for sure somebody from your office got over here to pick it up after Lucas found it there near the ballroom. Isn't that right?"

He has actually said 'Nope' a second time before he recognizes that she's speaking from knowledge. She escorts him to her chief's office, a glorified closet whose door is concealed artfully in the dark paneling, where they wait for her boss, Emilio, to dig the paperwork out of the file. What he presents to the judge is a pink copy of the triplicate returned property form that's used for items retrieved from

Lost and Found. On May 26, the day after George's cell phone turned up missing, John Banion signed for it.

George has already asked the doorman to call a taxi when he remembers Cassie and dashes back to the Salon. A huge brandy snifter of orange juice sits in front of her on the formal china.

He does not trust Cassie's discretion—she has virtually none—but he's mortified to think he suspected her, and the best excuse for meeting here is offered by the returned property form, which George, with some art, suggests he expected to be picking up.

"Huh," Cassie says as she studies it. "I thought it might be John."

"You did?"

"Only since yesterday afternoon. Marina came in to impound your computer."

"She didn't mention that," the judge says sourly, although in fairness to Marina, she probably regarded the need to seize the machine for evidence as obvious.

"John actually came in to ask her what she was

doing and why. I thought that was strange. Stranger." She gives her short blond hair a toss. "Frankly, George, I always wondered if the guy might be a secret ax murderer."

"Did you? I just assumed he was terribly lonely, Cassie."

She shrugs. The misfit, ungainly people of the world are not so much beneath her as incomprehensible. But George has faith in Cassie. She has infinite sympathy for the deprived. In time, she will recognize that suffering has many faces.

"I wonder if you have a clue what motivated him," George asks.

"He's not crazy about me."

"You're leaving."

"Right." She shrugs again. "I mean it's a crappy thing, George. But a guy like John—I wonder if he really can grab hold of how scary this was for you. You know, you're this judge, this mountain. I don't think he gets it."

The server puts their plates down before them. The food and the sad truth about Banion plunge them into silence.

As they start to eat, Cassie abruptly says, "I

should know you well enough to realize you didn't mean that stuff about an appetite for old sins." His heart squeezes at the prospect of her coming rebuke for his lack of faith in her, but instead she points at his plate. "No bacon," she says.

20

FORGIVEN

When the Judge and Cassie arrive at chambers a little
after nine, there are two problems. The first is that
he has no computer. The second is that John, who
is always at work by eight, has not appeared.

A technician from Information Services eventually comes up with what she swears is a clone of the
judge's machine. Predictably, it freezes the moment
the young woman is gone. George is still cursing
when Dineesha announces John's arrival.

George doubts that Dineesha knows exactly
what's going on—he's sworn Cassie to silence, a

vow that even she could not forsake so quickly—but Dineesha is intuitive enough to sense the disruption in the tiny universe of their chambers, especially since the judge has asked about Banion several times. In an oddly formal gesture, she ushers John in, her round face grave.

Banion, characteristically, cannot quite bring his eyes to the judge's. Instead he extends an envelope.

"What's this?" George asks.

"I've decided to resign, Your Honor. At the end of the term."

George hesitates to reach forward, realizing that he's been harboring some fragmentary hope that his conclusions about John would prove as unmerited as his suspicions of Cassie, one more misperception to be added to a list that has lately been growing impressively. But the meaning of John's desire to leave seems unambiguous: the search for #1 is over. Between them, silence lingers. It could be called meaningful, except that George has always experienced such moments with his clerk. In John's company, the question of who is supposed to speak next frequently seems to be a mystery to rival the beginnings of time.

"That's very disappointing, John. Sit down, please," the judge says. Banion has more or less lagged the letter onto George's desk and actually taken a step in the other direction. "What have you got lined up for yourself?"

At breakfast, George told Cassie that he wanted to handle things with John himself before involving Marina. But in the event, he's not sure what he means to accomplish. He has never been positive that confession by itself is good for the soul. Certainly, without a quid pro quo, it's seldom advantageous in the world of law—so many of George's clients ended up worse off for unburdening themselves by admitting what they'd done as soon as they were arrested. Nor does he have the heart to badger the truth from Banion. Cassie put her finger on it. It's a virtual certainty that John's actions were the product of his isolation, his inability to grasp the significance of his deeds to anybody but himself. That, of course, is the emotional synopsis of every crime. Which is why every crime, at its core, is marked by an element of pathos.

"I don't have anything, Judge. Not yet. There's a job as a staff clerk on the Alaska Supreme

Court that's been advertised. I might try for that."

"Alaska? Could you get any farther from here? Are you running away from somebody?"

Every trial lawyer tends to believe at moments that he is an actor worthy of Broadway, but George discovered in the courtroom that he has a limited range—quiet contempt for liars, an appealing dignity when beseeching juries to acquit. But he was never any good at broadcasting emotions he does not actually feel, and he has failed again now. He doesn't manage a convincing smile with the last words. Instead they emerge with a steely undertone of accusation, and that is all John needs. The soft face of forty-two-year-old John Banion crumples in upon itself like a rotting apple; he grows flush and, just like George's sons twenty-five years ago, begins to sob without control, initiating the same guilty, flustered moment when George is suddenly beyond his comfort zone in the world of adult justice.

"It's not me," John says then. "It's not me."

Against all reason, George finds his heart lighting up.

"Who then?" he asks. But John is crying too hard to hear him.

"It's not me to do something like this, Judge. It really isn't. It isn't."

John must repeat those words twenty times, continuing even after George has finally taken all this in and said more than once, "I know.

"I just don't understand *why*, John."

Banion gasps then. "That's why," he says and wails again.

"What's 'why'?"

"Because you didn't understand."

"What didn't I understand?"

"You made me *watch*!" John cries, stiffening in his vehemence. "You made me watch that awful, disgusting tape. You couldn't stand to see it, and so you made me watch it. *Me!* Ten times, twenty times, so I could describe all the most horrible things. It was disgusting!" Banion utters the last word with such fury he spits. Collapsed in the black wooden armchair in front of the judge's desk, he is a spitting, shaking, weeping mess. His skin is the color of a sunrise, and his face is wet all the way down to his chin. But he is a new man in George's eyes, not because he's crying—you couldn't deal with John without sensing sorrow. It's the depths of his anger that are shocking.

"How could you *do* that to me?" John is more or less shouting. That too is a novelty. "You didn't make *her* do it. But me? You didn't even ask if I'd mind. And you told me to watch it again and again." 'Her' is Cassie, of course. And Banion is right— right about a lot.

George drops his face into his hands for some time before finally turning to the window and peering down to the canopy of treetops in the parkway five floors below. No matter how equable and kind he aspires to be, how Christ-like in the way his father taught, he knows himself well enough to have predicted that his reaction to John was going to be anger. Worse, outrage. The sad man weeping in that chair betrayed the judge's trust, including by revealing himself as an outrageous nut. And he also committed a serious crime, wreaking havoc in George's life at a time when he was already on his heels.

But he feels very little of that. Instead, still his

father's son, he finds he is chastening himself. Because he failed mightily. He was too upset by his own secret crisis to consider anything besides escape. Knowing the profoundly disturbing quality of those images, he inflicted them on John without a second thought about the consequences. And the judge sees that his failures are not without their harsher ironies either. Pivoting under the weight of the bad old past, he nonetheless remained its captive; it was vestiges of old-fashioned chivalry that made him put aside any thought of asking Cassie to take on the task. And the truth, as John has clearly sensed, is that Cassie would have been far better equipped for the job. She might not have buffed her nails or microwaved a bag of popcorn while she watched, yet Cassie at some level is the worldliest person in these chambers when it comes to the subject of women and men. The tape would have infuriated her, fed her certainty about the proper outcome in the case. But she would have handled the tape far more calmly than John for one overriding reason: it would not have told her anything she had long tried to avoid knowing about the human universe—or herself.

"And you actually want to let those boys *go*," John cries. "You're willing to let them do all of that"—he is looking for a word, but it defies him— "all those terrible, terrible things, and you are actually thinking about letting them go when they have to be *punished*."

"John," Judge Mason says. He steps around his desk to comfort the man, but a protective pat on the shoulder is as far as he feels safe to go. "John, you should have said something."

"That was worse!" John heaves a gale and bawls harder. "Judge," he says, "Judge, I didn't want to disappoint you."

What sense do human beings ever make? George thinks. All of us. Each of us. The iron-headed logic of the law, which George has blithely mouthed, is that John should have spoken up. But to fully contemplate John's situation for a moment is to recognize how impossible that was. Could insular John Banion, so shocked and overwrought by what those images stimulated in him—could that man have admitted as much to anybody else? No wonder he felt certain that the judge would have been disappointed in him.

And there was one further rub: saying something would have required Banion to stop watching the video.

"John, I'm very sorry," the judge says and is struck at once by how much he means it. This is clearly the worst part: in his blindness, George has laid waste to a perfectly useful human being. Left to himself, John might have avoided forever what the judge forced him to confront. "Truly, John, I am sorry."

He realizes that there is probably not a word he can say that will be right, but his apology makes Banion howl again.

"Don't be noble!" he shouts. "You always want to be the best person. I'm the one who's sorry." The cycle plays out again here as it undoubtedly has in private for weeks: rage, then shame. Banion enters another prolonged period of weeping, then with his livid face and running eyes, suddenly looks straight at George for the first time.

"Forgive me," he says. "Please, forgive me. Can you forgive me, Judge?"

Forgiveness, George thinks. Confession alone might not be good for the soul. But forgiveness always is. What a slender, simple thing it is that has chased around these chambers for weeks like a yearning spirit.

"I forgive you, John," he says. "I do, I truly do." He pats John's shoulder one more time. Banion, in the chair, is now spinning his thin brown hair.

"I'm just no good at this," he tells the judge.

"At what?"

Banion weeps and weeps before he says, "At being a human being."

21

THE OPINION OF
THE COURT

NO. 94–1823

IN THE COURT OF APPEALS

FOR THE THIRD APPELLATE DISTRICT

People of the State	)	Appeal from the Superior
	)	Court of Kindle County
vs.	)	
	)	
Jacob I. Warnovits	)	
Kellen Cook Murphy	)	
Trevor Witt	)	
Arden Van Dorn	)	

Before Mason, Purfoyle and Koll, JJ.

Justice Mason delivered the Opinion of the Court:

This case comes before the Court on the appeal of the four defendants from their convictions on charges of criminal sexual assault and the resulting six-year penitentiary sentences imposed on them in the Superior Court of Kindle County. For the reasons stated below, this Court affirms.

As crimes so often do, this case has riled passions, broken hearts, and left behind a wake of lives forever disturbed. At its core, it asks us to reconsider a question the law has long pondered: how long, and under what circumstances, punishment may be delayed before the balance of justice tips against it?

[*Cassie, pls insert your draft's Statement of Facts here.*]

The statute of limitations in our state generally bars felony prosecutions brought more than three years after the crime. [*Cassie, fill in cite for the statute, please.*] The parties' briefs discuss at length the traditional policy considerations, which, from the recorded debates, appear to have influenced our legislature in creating this law:

recognitions that witnesses' memories dim with time; that a defense becomes more difficult to mount as evidence is dispersed; and that prompt prosecution maximizes deterrence and prevents the improperly motivated revival of long-ignored offenses. See e.g., *Toussie v. United States*, 397 U.S. 112, 114–115 (1970).

Yet as Justice Holmes taught us long ago, "The life of the law has not been logic; it has been experience." [*Pls chk quote and get cite. The Common Law?*] Statutes of limitations also recognize that human beings change with time. None of the familiar purposes of the criminal law—incapacitation, deterrence or retribution—are fully served by punishing those who have lived blamelessly over a considerable period since their crime, and so the law allows them to go forward without the anxiety of potential prosecution. [*Cassie, cite* Marion *case and various commentaries collected in Sapperstein's brief.*]

The precise circumstances under which prosecution is barred by the passage of time are a judgment left to the legislature. This Court's task is simply to assign to the statute's words the meanings its authors intended. [*cite cases*] Our legislators provided that the three-year limitations period is suspended while a defendant's affirmative steps to conceal his crime render the occurrence of the offense unknown. [*cite statute*] The defendants argue that this provision was wrongly applied in this case. They concede that the victim was unconscious when she was assaulted, but they maintain she knew enough from her physical condition in the aftermath to inform authorities that she had been raped. The conscientious trial judge, who heard the testimony on this question, disagreed. He found that, in light of the victim's age and experience, the defendants' concealment deprived her of a sufficient basis to make a credible report to authorities. The defendants deem that conclusion a reversible error of law, pointing out that another limitations exception is specifically addressed to underage victims, and that the provision would have barred this prosecution from being commenced. Accordingly, they contend that the victim's age was not a proper consideration here.

The question posed has not been decided pre-

viously by the higher courts of this state. Nonetheless, we do not see how a trial judge could
determine whether the defendants' concealment
prevented discovery of their crime without taking
into account all the attendant facts, including the
age and experience of the victim. It is a long rule
of the law that defendants must take their victims
as they find them. [*case citations*] These defendants were well aware of their victim's age and
the special advantages her naiveté might give
them in concealing their offense.

We are reinforced in our reading of the statute
of limitations by another consideration. To miti-
gate their offense, the defendants occasionally
note that the victim did not endure the grievous
psychological burdens of a rape because she was
unconscious at the time of the crime. This argument suffers not only from its temerity but also
from the fact that it proves too much. We credit
the victim's testimony that, as someone who was
still only nineteen years old and far from sea-
soned in life, she experienced considerable
trauma when she was finally forced to confront
what had happened four years before. In a very

real sense, the defendants' crime was not complete until that moment. We are sure that among
the legislature's motives for crafting this concealment provision was to reach offenses whose full
evil was not felt until their discovery.

We need not wonder in this case how long
prosecution might have been delayed by operation of the concealment provision before the limits of due process would require a different result.
[*citations*] The principal evidence of the offense,
the videotape, was in the custody of one of the
defendants until it was seized, and none of them
claim that it suffered any deterioration.[1] Nor is a
prosecution commenced three years and ten
months after the crime so distant in time as to
affront fundamental fairness. In fact, it is well
within the time allotted in other jurisdictions,
including the five-year limitations period followed
in the federal courts. [*cites*] Accordingly, we con-
clude that the defendants' prosecution was initi-
ated within the time limits provided by law.

[*Cassie: from here on in, use your draft with
my penciled changes.*]

[1] Our Brother Koll dissents, claiming that the videotape in fact was inadmissible under our state's eavesdropping law. [*citation*] This point was not raised in this Court or at trial, and thus we cannot consider it on our own, since we do not believe that admission of the tape, even assuming it might have been barred, allowed for a miscarriage of justice. We are driven to this conclusion by the real-world results of a decision to reverse on those grounds. Under our limitations provisions, the prosecution would have a year from the date of reversal to reindict the defendants for the eavesdropping offense, inasmuch as it was part of the same criminal transaction for which they were originally convicted. Since the tape could be admitted in that new case, conviction would be a virtual certainty. It does not strike us as a miscarriage of justice that the defendants were convicted of one felony rather than another, particularly because the underlying sexual assault could clearly be considered by the trial judge in aggravation of the sentence, making a significant prison term inevitable. Furthermore, it's quite likely that after a grant of immunity or plea bargains involving some of the defendants, one or more would be prosecuted for both eavesdropping *and* the rape, and could end up with an even longer sentence than the one imposed in this case. Any defendant who suffered that result would undoubtedly return to this court to complain about the miscarriage of justice caused by our meddling.

George has typed all of this with only his left hand. He briefly tried removing his right arm from the sling, but just a few keystrokes ignited pain all the way to his elbow. He takes the draft from the printer and walks it in to Cassie in the small clerks' office. She is eating an apple and takes another bite as she examines the first page.

"Surprised?" George asks.

"I knew whatever you decided would be okay, Judge." She calls him Judge no more than once a month, and thus he takes this as a testimonial. He asks her to give the draft priority, so that they can circulate it to Koll and Purfoyle tomorrow, in the hope of filing the opinion by the end of the week.

"Done before I leave tonight." She buffs her hands against each other. Thus spake Wonder Woman.

The sight of John's empty desk across from Cassie's remains evocative. He has been gone about three hours now. Dineesha helped him put everything in boxes. Then George came in to shake John's soft hand, a gesture the judge still regarded as appropriate after nine years of working together. Both the judge and the clerk were spent by their confrontation an hour before and said next to nothing at first.

'What's going to happen to me?' John finally asked at the door.

That is no small question. The imperatives are

the same as when he thought the culprit was Cassie: George cannot forgive this on his own. Marina, the county police, the FBI, and Bar Admissions and Discipline all have to be informed. John is facing a penitentiary term and loss of his law license at B.A.D.'s order. Now that his raging internal drama had leaked into the world of causes and effects, Banion appeared utterly bewildered.

'John, I'm afraid you should find a lawyer,' the judge said. That advice, unfortunately, constituted his good-bye.

With the *Warnovits* opinion out of his hands, and his tormentor dispatched, George feels the way he did years ago on the all-too-rare occasions when he won an acquittal. The sight of his client restored to freedom after the intense intellectual and physical exertion of the trial resounded not as evidence of justice—too often George knew the man was guilty—but as proof of the rattling power of his own will. In that mood, he became a whirlwind of high energy able to move through the mountain of neglected tasks that had arisen on his desk.

Now he trips downstairs to the chief file clerk for the court.

"I want to pick up my retention petition," George tells him. He fills out the single-page form on the spot, asking for two copies, one of which he carries up to the Chief Judge's secretary. Rusty, as it happens, sees George through the open door and waves him into his private chambers.

"Well, this is two pieces of good news in the same day," the Chief says, holding the petition.

"What's the other?"

"Nathan Koll resigned effective the end of term."

"You're kidding."

"He says no job is worth death threats. He carried on as if it were my fault. Wants me to arrange a year's police protection."

"You think he'll tell the cops where he lives or just ask them to blanket a mile-square sector?"

They laugh about Nathan.

"I'm afraid he doesn't have as much to fear as he thinks, Rusty."

As George explains about John, the Chief falls into a chair.

"What in the hell?" he finally asks. "What could he possibly have been thinking?"

"It's the usual goofy story," George replies. "The more John watched the tape, the more wound up he got, and the more he blamed me for making him do it. He was in that state one day when I stepped out for a second and on impulse he went to my computer and sent the first e-mail to some nonexistent address, knowing it would bounce back and appear on my screen."

"'You'll pay'?"

"'You'll pay.' After he'd done it, he had second thoughts, especially about getting caught. How many people could possibly have had access to my machine? So when I was out again, he erased the original message, and the copy in my Sent file, and then, in order to deflect attention from the message that had come from my computer, he resent it twice from his own through an open relay server.

"And that was basically the cycle. Raging, acting out, then remorseful and afraid of getting nabbed. Of course, I was too distracted about Patrice to pay much attention at first, which only honked John off worse and made the next messages more pointed."

"And where was he when he was doing this?"

"He says he sent almost all of the messages from his laptop while he was in his office, maybe forty feet from me."

"Help me here," Rusty says. "Isn't this the clerk who saw one of the early messages and told you to call Court Security?"

"Sure, he'd sent it, and while it was crossing the Internet he walked in to watch my reaction."

"But why did he tell you to bring in Marina?"

"Well, first of all, he *wanted* me to be scared. He had to act as if we'd seen the reaper. And what better cover than to be the one who says 'Call the cops'?"

Rusty gives a bitter snort: people.

"The other thing," George says, "that really lit John's fuse was the idea that I might let those kids get off. He was desperate for big-time punishment."

"Teach me a lesson," Rusty says, "by teaching them. Who says there's no point to vengeance?"

The two friends by now are sitting side by side in wooden armchairs in the center of the Chief's vast chambers and exchange the same rueful smile.

"Anyway," George says, "as I kept giving him assignments on the case, John realized that I was bothered about the limitations question. Apparently, I said as much to him on the day of oral argument. That's what inspired the death-watch message. And after the conference, Purfoyle's clerk told him I seemed pretty serious about reversing. So he notched it up again and sent that e-mail to my home. But nothing flipped him out like talking to me face-to-face. There I was, this fellow he used to admire, ready to free the devil's minions. So he got out his nuke. He had my cell phone by then."

"And how did he get his hands on it?"

Apparently, George says, he'd dropped the cell in the rear corridor outside the Gresham's ballroom. Hotel security found it the next day and called Banion, because he'd inquired only a few hours before on the judge's behalf.

"John said he was always on the verge of giving it back and claiming the hotel had just found it, but he was already sending messages by then. I'm sure that as soon as he picked up the phone, he realized it would give him a great new way to scare the bejesus out of me."

The Chief rakes a hand through his graying hair as he ponders.

"You think this guy hears voices, Georgie?"

"I think he's a troubled, lonely guy. And I hit his crazy bone."

"He would have gone off sooner or later."

"I just don't know." That will remain the hardest part for George. "He told me I always want to be the best person."

"Imagine that," says his old friend.

"And that he was afraid to disappoint me."

The Chief takes a second to consider George. He has not lost his good humor, but he has stopped smiling in favor of a one-eyed squint.

"George, this was not your fault."

"I could have—"

"No," says the Chief. "Sainthood is not required. You're entitled to some limitations."

George could say more. But Rusty, a rigorous man of the law, will never see this from anything but a legal perspective, which deems John a criminal and everyone else blameless. The two are silent for a second, each man with his own thoughts.

"Okay," Rusty says eventually, "I understand why your clerk figured *you* did him wrong. But why start picking on Koll?"

"Oh," says George. He'd forgotten that part. "The more John ratcheted up the threats, the more scared he was of the consequences. You've seen this weather pattern: daring to get caught, afraid he'll get caught, afraid he won't. The staff knew that Marina and the Bureau weren't getting anywhere in their investigation. But the one suspicion I'd asked her to keep to herself was about Corazón—just to damp down any hysteria. When John sat in on that meeting with Marina and realized how committed she was to nailing Corazón, he became convinced he could skate. So he tried to gin up a little more evidence. He remembered that Koll had been on Corazón's panel. And, given John's feelings about reversing *Warnovits*, he was happy to stick it to Nathan anyway."

"There you have it," Rusty says about the threat to Koll, "it's a law of nature. Even the bubonic plague did some good."

"But now John was trying to do impressions of a gangbanger. Which was why that message looked like seventh grade."

"He didn't have anything to do with those thugs in the garage, did he?"

"That one's all on me. I was trying to pee on peril, just to show myself I wasn't scared. In a better frame of mind, I'd have recognized that those kids were marking me."

"Will you promise that, from now on, you'll cool out in the corner of a bar like an average human being?"

"No way. I'm sticking with the garage. I'm hoping for a big workmen's comp claim." George lifts the sling.

"You may run into some trouble on appeal," the Chief says.

"Anyway, when Marina came in to impound the computer, she must have given John a hint that it was about the very first message, and he knew that would be the end."

"Because?"

"Because Marina would focus on my staff. Sooner or later, with that group under suspicion, she'd reinvestigate the way they looked for the cell phone. And besides, it wouldn't take a nightstick and a bright light for John to wilt under questioning."

"Speaking of Marina, have you told her all this yet?"

"She's called four times. But I want John to get a lawyer first."

"Oh, thank you," the Chief says, "thank you for that. Five will get you ten that I'll have a letter by the end of the week threatening all of us with a suit for a hostile workplace. Simon Legree was employer of the year compared to you, making poor John watch that terrible videotape over and over again."

"You think that'll give him a little leverage?"

Rusty bobs his head this way and that. "A little. We've both seen screwier defenses. So what do you want him to get, Mr. Justice Bleeding-Heart?"

"I don't see the point of prosecution. The guy's forty-two years old, no record, great service to the court. I hope the P.A. agrees to a diversion program with psychiatric treatment."

"And what are those boys who held you up going to catch?"

"Those boys have had their second chance. And their twelfth. And Banion didn't break my arm. Or pull a gun."

"And what about his license?"

"Suspended. Until his shrink says otherwise. Any chance you can support all of that, Rusty? I'm sure Marina will want the death penalty."

"I'm sure. But only after your clerk spends several months at Abu Ghraib." Rusty mulls, eyeing the distance. "Diversion is still confidential, isn't it?"

"Right."

"And the suspension. That's a one-liner in the court record. Nobody knows why."

"Right. What are you thinking, Chief?"

"I'm thinking John Banion's a fortunate guy."

"Because?"

"Because I want this to go away quietly. Very quietly. I'm going to put Marina on an investigative moratorium. For the good of the court. When John's lawyer calls, you can tell her or him to try to work this out on a double-deep, supersecret, confidential basis with the P.A. and Bar Admissions. Along the lines you mentioned. With my consent. I'll repeat that to whoever needs to hear it."

"Thank you, Rusty."

"I'd let you kiss my ring, but the truth, chum, is that I'm doing this for all of us. I don't want Koll to hear this story, not before the ink is completely dry on his resignation. And the County Board's going to vote on Marina's funding request within the next week. Better they don't start thinking that everything with #1 was just a little soap opera in your chambers and get second thoughts about giving us the money."

"The wisdom of power." George stands.

"May I ask?"

"What's that?"

"About *Warnovits*," says Rusty. "Is it decided?"

"I have a draft."

"Was justice done?" After his performance last week, Rusty is reluctant to ask directly whether the case is being affirmed or reversed until the opinion is public. And just now, as a matter of friendly torment, George chooses not to answer. Instead, Judge Mason places his good hand on the head of his friend in brief, mutual benediction.

"We try," George says. "We can only try."

Visit **www.panmacmillan.com** to read more about all our books and to buy them. You will also find features, author interviews and news of any author events, and you can sign up for **e-newsletters** so that you're always first to hear about our new releases.

www.panmacmillan.com

GIFT SELECTOR
YOUR ACCOUNT
WISH LIST
WAITING LIST

HOME | ABOUT US | IMPRINTS | TRADE/MEDIA | CONTACT US | ADVANCED SEARCH | SEARCH | GO

BOOK CATEGORIES | WHAT'S NEW | AUTHORS/ILLUSTRATORS | BESTSELLERS | READING GROUPS

Coming Soon...

Reading Groups

Competitions
Feeling Lucky?

Extracts
Sneak Previews

Interviews

Events
Meet Our Stars

Reviews
What The Critics Say

News & Awards

Editor's Choice
What We're Reading